ORION'S MESSENGER

by

Antonia de Winter

**Grosvenor House
Publishing Limited**

This book is published by
Grosvenor House Publishing Ltd
Link House
140 The Broadway, Tolworth, Surrey, KT6 7HT.
www.grosvenorhousepublishing.co.uk

A CIP record for this book
is available from the British Library

ISBN 978-1-83975-182-0

Dedications

For Reuben, Doren, Amélie and Zion
Let your imagination fly...
With love,
Oma

Acknowledgements

My golden acknowledgement goes to Howard for lending an ear to my ideas and listening to the unfolding story with unusual patience. Your constructive suggestions and grammatical eloquence (not to mention your talented voice box) have been invaluable. Also and most welcomed, for making cups of tea at the right time!

An important thank you to the person who knows who they are, for setting the ball rolling again and being so helpful with technical know-how.

To Vanessa, Lorrine and Raglan. You have been there with me on this winding road, and your support along the way has been much appreciated.
Most recently to Alistair for your insightful advice.
A Big Thank You To You All.

CONTENTS

Chapter 1.
How It All Started

The ghost train rolled slowly into the dark tunnel. Alex was sitting in an open carriage and he shivered as a damp mist swirled around him. He felt frightened and excited at the same time because he didn't know what to expect. Wolves howled in the distance as the train picked up speed and clattered along the track. Suddenly, a large black spider dangled in front of his face and made him jump. "Oh no!" he shrieked. A moment later some ghostly white figures leapt out in front of him, wailing and moaning, "Woo-oo-oo-oo!" As the figures faded into the darkness, he thought, " Whatever is going to happen next?"

The ghost train gathered speed and swayed wildly around the bends. Alex's eyes were screwed tightly shut and he hung on as best he could. "This must be the craziest thing I've ever done!" he muttered. All of a sudden, he heard the brakes screeching and the train slowed down, finally emerging from the eerie surroundings of the dark tunnel. Alex opened his eyes again and blinked in the bright sunlight as the ghost train ground to a halt at the end of the track. He climbed down from the train and was aware of somebody talking to him.

"Alex, Alex are you listening to me?" He shook his head to clear away the daydream and realised he was sitting in the kitchen at home. His mother was trying to catch his attention, but he had drifted away, remembering the best day of his school holidays. It was springtime and he'd been taken to the funfair by his parents. What a brilliant time he'd had riding on the merry-go-round, crashing the bumper cars and whizzing down the helter-skelter. He'd even won a huge blue teddy bear on the coconut shy stall but, best of all, was that ride on the ghost train. It had all been great fun. But now, here he was, sitting at the kitchen table with his mother talking to him about boring everyday stuff. He drifted off again, thinking about the rest of his holiday, which had been uneventful and so disappointing.

For a start, his big sister Clare had gone to visit their grandparents in the countryside. They lived in a 400-year-old farmhouse in Rutland, grew all their own vegetables and had llamas grazing in the field behind the house. Clare enjoyed staying with them, doing the sorts of things she didn't get to do as a 'townie', like climbing the trees in the orchard or maybe picking tomatoes in the greenhouse and sometimes even helping to feed the llamas. That was why she had not been around to keep Alex company for the whole of the spring holiday.

Alex thought the house seemed empty without Clare. Usually, music could be heard drifting from her bedroom or he could hear the sound of her voice on the phone chatting with her friends. But now everything was strangely quiet.

Alex's best friend Reuben had gone away too, staying with his cousins down by the coast. Alex really missed Reuben because he lived close by and, usually, they went to the park together to play football after school.

His other good pal, Manny, was stuck indoors with a nasty cold and Alex hadn't seen him at all, not even on the day he'd gone to the funfair.

Then there was Amelou, the girl who lived next door and was oh-so bright and chatty. Amelou could kick a ball around in the back garden just as well as any boy, but even that had not happened recently because it just kept on raining. Only one day had been sunny and warm. Luckily, that had been the day of the funfair when Alex came back with the blue teddy bear he'd won. He hadn't known what to do with it – and so he gave it to Amelou.

The holiday was drawing to a close and, for once, he was pleased to be going back to school. He was half listening to his mother, as she carried on talking to him about tidying his bedroom, doing some shopping, and blah, blah, blah, when suddenly his ears perked up.

"By the way, I've just had a surprise phone call from dear Aunt Melissa. She wants to take you to the Great Museum of History this afternoon, Alex. Now isn't that nice?"

"Yes Mum" said Alex, with no excitement in his voice. Then he thought, "I've never been to a museum before. Really not sure I want to go, especially not with Aunt Melissa."

Well 'dear Aunt Melissa', as his mother called her, was a curious lady with a brusque manner. And what a sight she was to behold – with plenty of copper-coloured curls sticking out from underneath her favourite green felt hat and a pair of pointy black-rimmed spectacles dangling from a silver chain around her neck. On her mouth was smeared a dazzling red lipstick, making her look like a pantomime dame. Nobody was allowed to disagree with Aunt Melissa, as she was a very 'knowing person', having spent hours in the library reading up on subjects like 'Countries of the World' and 'Creatures Great and Small'. Her favourite saying was, "Well, I certainly know what I'm talking about."

Aunt Melissa lived in a quaint terraced house filled with tortoiseshell and marmalade cats. The place was scattered with china teapots and cut-glass vases filled with dried flowers that had been there for many years. Faded lace curtains hung at the windows, casting a pale sunlight over her dusty living room. Her cats would snuggle into tartan blankets on the squashy worn sofa, which was so big it took up most of the room. Whenever Alex visited Aunt Melissa for tea, he wanted to cover his ears because, in that shrill voice of hers, she rattled on endlessly about everything and nothing at all. Anyway, Aunt Melissa had offered to take him to the museum and that had to be slightly better than wandering around the house aimlessly.

The morning seemed a little brighter now, even though his mother insisted on taking him to the supermarket first. He wasn't quite as grumpy as he might have been, zooming up and down the aisles for packets of pasta and washing powder to put in the trolley, which was soon filled. Luckily, the supermarket wasn't very busy so they moved quickly through the checkout.

Back home again, Alex helped unpack the shopping as his mother made lunch. He hurriedly ate mouthfuls of fish fingers and baked beans and had just cleared his plate when the doorbell rang. Alex's mother opened the front door and there stood Aunt Melissa. She looked extremely colourful in a flowing cape of violet mauve

5

and, as usual, her favourite green felt hat was sitting on a mass of copper-coloured curly hair. Today she was wearing a lipstick that was as bright a red as you'd find in a punnet of strawberries.

"My goodness, she looks just like a witch!" thought Alex.

His aunt didn't even say hello.

"Are we ready to go?" she demanded, peering down at him through her black-rimmed specs.

"Yes, Aunt Melissa," he replied, grabbing his jacket.

"Have a good time and enjoy yourselves," said Alex's mother, as she stood on the doorstep and watched them walk down the road towards the bus stop.

Chapter 2.

An Outing To Remember

Alex and Aunt Melissa sat on the top deck of the bus heading towards the Great Museum of History. Alex looked out of the window at the people walking by with their umbrellas up, as Aunt Melissa wittered on about the antics of her precious cats.

It didn't take long to get to the museum and once they'd stepped off the bus, Alex looked at the imposing grey building in front of him.

"Gosh, it's even bigger than I imagined," he thought.

Aunt Melissa marched up the stone steps and through the huge carved wooden doors, with Alex following close behind. Aunt Melissa bought tickets at the entrance and they approached the turnstile. Once inside the museum, Alex immediately spotted a souvenir counter and started walking towards it.

"Not now Alex, we'll have time to look at all those things later!" said Aunt Melissa sharply.

She took him to a gigantic plan of the museum that was displayed on a wall and studied it carefully for a minute or two.

"Hmm, where shall we go first? I know, this looks interesting," she said, pointing her bony finger towards a sign that read 'Creatures of the Past.'

She walked briskly along the corridor and up the main staircase, Alex hot on her heels. At the top of the stairs was a display of huge dinosaur skeletons and Alex's eyes nearly popped out of his head at the sight in front of him.

"Wow! Just look at the size of those *enormous* creatures! Earth must have been a very frightening place to live in, millions of years ago," he exclaimed.

Aunt Melissa ignored his comment and said in her usual 'knowing' manner, "Now over here is the Pterodactyl."

Alex stared at the gigantic beast that was towering above them and thought to himself, "I'll bet that dinosaur could have eaten a whole tree in one mouthful and roared loud enough to take the roof off this museum!" Then he said out loud, "I must come here again, but next time I'll bring Clare, Reuben, Manny and Amelou, because they won't believe what I've just seen!"

He would happily have spent the whole afternoon wandering in and out of the dinosaurs, but it was not to be, as Aunt Melissa hurried him along to the next grand hall.

"Historical Costumes from 200 to 300 years ago," announced Aunt Melissa, reading the sign on the door. Inside were many doll-like mannequins and models, wearing clothes from centuries past. There were ladies in beautiful silk embroidered dresses, with sparkling jewels and pearls around their necks. They peered out from behind fans of feathers and lace and gazed at the people passing by.

The gentlemen wore heavy velvet jackets, trousers called 'knee breeches' and wigs made out of long, dark wavy hair. Alex thought they looked very uncomfortable.

Moving along, a boy mannequin dressed in clothes from days gone by, stared out at Alex. He was wearing a white shirt with lace ruffles down the front and brown corduroy knee breeches. On his head sat a three-cornered hat called a 'tricorn', similar to the hat worn by the Lord Mayor of London. On his feet were black leather shoes with big shiny buckles on the front.

"How on earth did he play football dressed like that?" asked Alex.

"Don't be ridiculous Alex! They didn't play football in those days," retorted Aunt Melissa.

"I'll bet they did," he said under his breath. He felt pleased to be living in the present day and lucky enough to put on clothes that were soft and easy to wear, unlike all that stiff and heavy clothing from the olden days.

"Alex, come along, I think we'll visit the Great Hall of Wonders next," said Aunt Melissa and abruptly she marched along the corridor with Alex trying to keep up. The archway before them opened into another splendid hall. With a roof made of clear glass, everything looked light and bright. The hall was filled with huge statues and other items from around the world. Alex went over to where a colourful totem pole stood. It was carved out of a single enormous tree trunk and had brightly coloured bird heads and motifs painted all around it. He gazed at it with curiosity and saw that it was over 100 years old and came from Alaska in the north west of America.

In another area was a grand Egyptian sphinx made from limestone, its face worn away by wind and desert sand over many thousands of years. Alex read what it said below. 'A sphinx is a mythical creature with the head of a man and the body of a lion.'

"How strange is that," thought Alex.

Next to the sphinx and carved in white marble, a stately Roman emperor stood in his great chariot and he was waving to the crowds. Alex imagined he could almost hear the crowds chanting at this impressive spectacle.

Then something caught his eye in the middle of the Great Hall of Wonders and Alex walked up to take a closer look. It was a magnificent bronze falcon with its wings spread as if ready for flight. It looked very real – Alex felt he could almost touch the bird's enchanting feathers. With mysterious eyes like black diamonds staring right out at him, he thought this bird was most magical and fantastic. He took a few steps back and continued to gaze at the wonderful vision. Aunt Melissa came over to him and then read the plaque below the falcon.

'Orion's Messenger – From a Place and Time Unknown.'

"What does that mean Aunt Melissa?" queried Alex.

Well, for once Aunt Melissa wasn't all knowing.

"It appears I cannot tell you anything about this falcon, except that his name is Orion's Messenger."

"How on earth do they know his name if they don't know where he comes from?" asked Alex.

"That's a very good question," said his aunt, who was becoming more irritated by the moment. She turned around and spotted a museum attendant leaning up against the doorway.

"Good afternoon, would you be good enough to tell us more about the statue in the middle of the hall?" she piped.

"You'll be meaning Orion's Messenger, Ma'am. I wish I could tell you as much about 'im as I can about the others. The truth of the matter is, I can't tell you anything

at all. People comes from far an' wide to see 'im, and 'ees much admired, but it's a real mystery 'ow 'ee came to be 'ere. Sorry I can't 'elp you any more than that, Ma'am," said the attendant, doffing his cap at her.

"Oh dear and tish tosh!" exclaimed Aunt Melissa. This was the first time during their visit that she hadn't been able to impress Alex with her knowledge and she snapped at him, "We've spent enough time in this hall so let's move on now!" She turned to the attendant once again, "Direct us to the Antique Clock Hall, would you?!"

"That-a-way, Ma'am," he said, pointing to a walkway close by and wished for the hundredth time that he knew more about the mysterious statue called Orion's Messenger.

Aunt Melissa strode off and Alex was none too pleased at having to leave the Great Hall of Wonders – but where Aunt Melissa went Alex had to follow. She led him into a smaller hall with a dark ceiling and a strong smell of polished wood. The constant sound of tick-tock and striking chimes filled the air from a vast array of old time pieces. Tall grandfather clocks with swinging pendulums lined the walls next to gilded clocks surrounded by cherubs and delicate flowers. On display behind glass cases were some clocks so small they were almost the size of a large watch but covered in coloured enamel and precious jewels. They even had skeleton clocks, which allowed Alex to see quite clearly inside the clocks and also showed how they worked.

This hall was not as amazing as the Great Hall of Wonders or as exciting as the hall with all the dinosaurs. But Alex was surprised that clocks came in so many different shapes and sizes. He thought he would never look at the kitchen clock in the same way ever again!

After a while, Aunt Melissa tapped him on the shoulder.

"My feet are aching, Alex, I think we've seen enough for today, so let's go home now," she grumbled. And, before he had a chance to say anything, she took his arm and together they marched out of the Antique Clock Hall and down the central staircase towards the front entrance. On the way out, Alex spotted the souvenir stall.

"Oh, Aunt Melissa, please may I buy something from the museum as a memento to take home," he asked.

"All right but be quick about it!" she snapped.

He dashed over to the counter and looked at what was on display. There was a selection of picture postcards of the dinosaurs, historical costumes, and the antique clocks. Then there were assorted colouring pencils saying things like, 'I've Visited the Great Museum of History,' or 'I've just seen a Pterodactyl!' Books, jigsaws, maps and more... So much choice – it was difficult for Alex to make up his mind. But then he spotted exactly what he wanted. For there, hanging up on the wall behind the counter, was a big colour poster of the bronze falcon – Orion's Messenger.

"That's it!" he exclaimed in an excited voice, pointing to the poster, "That's just what I want, Aunt Melissa."

"Why on earth would you want something so large Alex? Now come along and choose something more sensible." said his Aunt in her very shrill voice.

"But Aunt Melissa...," started Alex.

"No buts, and hurry up, otherwise we'll miss the next bus home!" screeched Aunt Melissa.

Alex was filled with dismay. "I don't see anything else I really want," he said glumly.

"Suit yourself, then we'll be off!"

And, with that, she turned on her heel and led him briskly out of the museum.

The bus ride home was not very pleasant. Aunt Melissa wouldn't stop talking about things she'd seen in the museum.

"Well, now I *know* more about the totem poles of north west America and…" Blah, blah, blah, she wittered on and on. Alex looked out of the bus window, upset at what had just happened. He would have been so happy to round off the afternoon with that super poster tucked under his arm. But sadly it was not to be.

Once home, Alex slipped inside the house as Aunt Melissa stood on the front doorstep talking to his mother. "I'm sure Alex has learnt quite a lot from his visit to the museum today," she commented and then said impatiently, "No thank you, I won't come in for tea as I have to get home and feed my dear cats." And, with that, and a whirl of her violet flowing cape, she was gone.

A little later, when Alex was tucking into a plate of tasty chicken nuggets, chips and his favourite sweet corn, he told his mother about the afternoon he'd spent with Aunt Melissa. He described all the fascinating things he'd seen in the museum, including the statue of Orion's Messenger in the Great Hall of Wonders. He also mentioned the unhappy incident at the souvenir counter when Aunt Melissa had not let him have that poster.

His mother listened with care and asked him questions about the dinosaurs, the historical costumes and the antique clocks too.

"My, my, what an interesting afternoon you've had. But I think Aunt Melissa was a bit unfair for not letting you have that poster. As it's the last day of your holiday tomorrow, perhaps we'll pop back to the museum and buy it. Would you like that Alex?"

Alex couldn't believe his luck. His mother wanted to take him back to the museum just to pick up the poster. "Oh yes please!" he exclaimed.

"It'll be our secret," she winked at him.

The afternoon had ended well after all and it wasn't long before it was time for bed. Happy and content, Alex snuggled down under the covers and soon he fell fast asleep.

It was much later, and the night sky was very black, when Alex woke up with a jolt! He rubbed his eyes and wondered why he had woken up so suddenly. He thought about it for a moment and then realised. Somebody had been calling his name. He listened earnestly in the darkness, but there was total silence. He slipped out of bed and tiptoed along the corridor. He could hear his mother and father gently snoring behind their bedroom door, so it couldn't have been either of them. He shrugged his shoulders and clambered back into bed again and thought, "I must have been dreaming," as he drifted off to sleep once more.

Chapter 3.
A Raging Storm

The following morning brought the delicious smell of melted cheese on toast wafting up from the kitchen. Still in his pyjamas, Alex quickly slid down the bannisters before anyone saw him.

"Good morning, Alex," said his father, sitting at the table and eating a bowl of cornflakes.

"Morning, Dad, you'll never guess what happened to me last night," answered Alex.

"Oh, and what was that?" he asked, only half-listening.

"It was very strange. I woke up in the middle of the night because I thought someone was calling my name," he said sounding puzzled.

His father stopped eating and looked up at him curiously.

"How odd, perhaps we have ghosts in the house!" he chuckled.

Alex's mother sat down at the table with the cheesy toast and a cup of tea.

"Don't you go putting strange ideas into Alex's head. Everybody knows there are no such things as ghosts! I'm sure it was just a dream, that's all."

"Whatever it was, it didn't keep me awake as I went straight back to sleep," said Alex, as he poured some Cocoa Ping-Pongs into a cereal bowl.

This was the very last day of Alex's school holiday and he was feeling good because he was going back to the Great Museum of History. He bolted down his breakfast and got dressed quickly. Then he walked up and down the corridor waiting impatiently for his mother to get ready too.

It wasn't long before Alex and his mother went out of the front door and ran for the bus, with umbrellas up again to shield them from today's downpour. Soon they were once more on the grey stone steps of the museum.

"This way," he said, as he guided his mother through the huge old entrance. Once inside, she shook the rain off her umbrella and gazed around. Alex took her over to the souvenir counter.

"Come and see what I was telling you about," he said with excitement. Before she had a chance to look at anything else, Alex pointed to the large colour poster on the wall. With a grand gesture he announced proudly, "*This* is Orion's Messenger."

Alex's mother was pleasantly surprised as she studied the splendid looking bird in front of her.

"Well, Alex, I can't think why Aunt Melissa wouldn't let you have such a colourful poster. We're here now, so let's buy it."

She beckoned to the friendly assistant, who was dressed from head to toe in candy pink. Even her trainers and the scrunchie in her blond ponytail were pink! Miss Candy Pink was standing behind the counter as Alex's mother pointed to the wall, "We'd like to buy that poster please."

"You're in luck, It's the only one we have left," said Miss Candy Pink.

Alex watched eagerly as Miss Candy Pink climbed onto the step stool to remove the poster. Then she rolled it carefully before wrapping it up in brown paper. She handed it to Alex with a smile, "You'd better put this somewhere special."

"Oh, I will!" he replied enthusiastically, and he took the package from her and said goodbye.

Alex's mother turned to him, "What a shame we can't stay for a while. I'm expecting a delivery at home shortly and I really don't want to find a package sitting on the doorstep. However, I promise we shall come back one day in the future and spend a lot more time looking around the museum, Alex."

"Thanks, Mum! And next time I'd like to bring my friends with me too," he said happily.

They arrived home just in time to see the delivery man walking along the garden path. Whilst his mother took in the parcel, Alex belted up the stairs to the top of the house.

"Can I put the poster in the loft, Mum?" he shouted down.

"I don't see why not," she said, as she took off her coat.

He'd been using the loft as his playroom for a while now. It was an open area, with a skylight window that dimly lit up the dark wooden rafters. Scattered about were broken suitcases, toys and junk from the past, which his parents couldn't bear to throw away. Alex stepped forward on the bare floorboards, and carefully climbed over an old-fashioned vinyl record player and a dusty, rusty baby pram. He searched in the half-light until he found the perfect spot for his poster. Standing on tiptoes, he reached up and fixed it between the rafters. He took a step back.

"That looks just right!" he said out loud.

Then, he peered into the gloomy loft looking for something to sit on.

Rummaging around, he found an old dining chair and placed it in front of the poster. He turned the chair back to front and sat astride the seat. Cupping his chin in his hands he leant forward. He was in his own special place and there was no one there to disturb him. He sat gazing at the bird and he let his imagination run away with him.

"Just look at you and your incredible wings. I'll bet you could fly to the moon and back without being tired. And what about those deep, dark mysterious eyes of yours? What have you seen that will remain a secret forever?"

The poster had the very same words that were written on the statue in the museum. 'Orion's Messenger – From a Place and Time Unknown.'

"Where oh where did you come from?" thought Alex to himself. "Perhaps from a little island surrounded by sparkling blue waters, where the sun shines all year around. Yes, he could imagine it quite clearly. An enchanted place far, far away... He became so busy with his own thoughts that he didn't realise how quickly time was slipping by. Eventually, he heard footsteps and his mother appeared in the doorway.

"Have you put the poster up? Oh yes, you have!" she said looking at the giant falcon staring down at them. She clambered over an old trunk to take a closer look. She studied the picture carefully and, after a pause, she said, "I don't know what it is, but there is something very special about that bird. I've never seen one quite like it before."

"Orion's Messenger is more than special, he is truly magnificent!" said Alex nodding his head in agreement.

"That may be so, Alex, but you've spent enough time up here daydreaming. Do you have everything that you need in your schoolbag for tomorrow?"

"Oh my goodness!" He was so wrapped up in his own world that he had completely forgotten about school. He rose slowly from his chair and took a long, last wistful look at Orion's Messenger. Then he scrambled over the junk and left the loft, carefully closing the door behind him.

After supper that evening, as Alex climbed into bed, his father popped his head around the door and said, "You're in bed a bit early, aren't you?"

"I suppose so, but I don't mind for once. I'm really looking forward to seeing my friends tomorrow."

"I'll switch off the light then and I hope you sleep tight." As his father was halfway out of the door, he stopped and turned around.

"I'm sure you won't be hearing any more of those strange voices like you did last night."

"Hopefully not. Goodnight, Dad," said Alex settling down.

His father gently pulled the door to. Alex lay his head on the pillow and shut his eyes. He could hear rain falling, plip, plop, plip, plop, as it dripped off the tree onto his window ledge. Pulling the duvet up over his ears, it wasn't long before he fell fast asleep.

Suddenly, there was an enormous crash of thunder and Alex opened his eyes with a start! The gently falling rain had turned into a raging storm. Branches of the tree outside whipped loudly against his window and the thunder roared overhead. He must have been asleep for hours because the time on the clock showed nearly midnight. Once more he listened to the wind whistling around the house.

"A-l-e-x, A-l-e-x..."

Alex sat bolt upright! Was that the wind howling or was someone actually calling his name? A minute passed and Alex began to believe it was just his imagination. He listened as furious raindrops hurtled down from the sky and fell noisily against his windowpane. More thunder boomed! Another minute passed as the storm slowly rolled on and the crashing and banging started to fade a little. Alex decided that his imagination was getting the better of him and he started to slide down under the covers. Just as he was shutting his eyes – there it was again.

"A-l-e-x, A-l-e-x."

It sounded like a long, low eerie whisper. Alex was in no doubt now – someone *was* calling his name! He slipped out of bed and opened his bedroom door. He wasn't sure if it was a good idea but he peeped out cautiously. There were only shadows, still he decided to walk along the corridor past his parents' bedroom. Not a sound could be heard, not even snoring this time. Suddenly, lightening flashed down from the top of the stairs leading to the loft. But how could that be? He remembered quite clearly that he had shut the loft door behind him earlier. Lightening streaked again and brought momentary daylight to the hallway.

"Is it possible that someone is up there?" He felt alarmed but then said very softly under his breath, "I'd better go and take a look."

As quiet as a mouse, he started to tiptoe up the stairs, avoiding the creaky step so as not to wake anyone up. When he got to the top, slowly he pushed the door open...

Chapter 4.

Journey To A Different Place

Alex took a deep breath before peering around the loft door and into the darkness. At that very moment lightening flashed again. He gasped with surprise and clutched his hand to his mouth.

"Crumpets and trumpets. Oh my!" he spluttered.

"Don't be afraid, Alex," said a softly spoken voice.

The room was in dark shadows once more.

"I must be seeing things," whispered Alex under his breath.

"I've been calling you for such a long time," said the Voice.

There was another flash of lightening, this time with a loud clap of thunder. It nearly made Alex jump out of his skin!

"I can't believe what I'm seeing. Is it *really* you?" he gasped.

"Oh yes, I assure you I am quite real," said the Voice

Alex was shaking as he stuttered, "I – I – I don't understand..."

"Come closer Alex," said the Voice.

Alex took two hesitant steps forward. Another flash of lightening lit up the loft brilliantly. Alex's eyes became as big as saucers for there, perched on the back of the old dining chair, was an *enormous* bird.

"Who, who … who are you?" he asked, but he knew the answer already.

"I am Orion's Messenger, of course," said the bird in a matter-of-fact way.

"But-but-but you're talking," stammered Alex.

"You thought I was a magical bird, and you're quite right," said the falcon.

It was all too much for Alex to take in. "I- I -I saw you in the museum – and now you're here… But why?" he asked in a bewildered voice.

"I am here because of you," came the calm reply.

"What on earth do you mean?" asked Alex. He wasn't frightened anymore, but he pinched himself to make sure he wasn't dreaming.

"Time is short and there is little I can tell you. Just trust me when I say your help is needed," said the falcon.

"I really don't understand. And why me?" questioned Alex.

"That I cannot say but you will find out more if you come now. I must leave soon, Alex. Will you fly with me?" Orion's Messenger invited him urgently.

"But, but I have school tomorrow," said Alex.

"Don't concern yourself with that. Time stands still where we are going and nobody will *ever* know you've been gone," said the falcon.

It didn't take a moment for Alex to realise that this could be the adventure of a lifetime. He turned to the falcon and said in a clear voice, "Yes, I will go with you."

"Good, I was hoping you would agree," said Orion's Messenger.

"What happens now?" asked Alex.

"Go and put on some warm clothes, then creep into the back garden and stand by the plum tree. I shall meet you there very soon. Now hurry, hurry!" urged the falcon.

Alex returned to his bedroom and quickly changed into a warm grey shirt and a pair of jeans. He slipped into his trainers and put on a cosy blue hoody. By the time he'd crept into the garden, the storm had passed over and the soft light of the moon was peeping out from behind a cloud. Alex did as he'd been instructed and stood on the path by the plum tree. Soon he heard the flutter of feathers in the air and watched as Orion's Messenger gently landed on the grass.

"Alex, it's time to fly, so hold on tight," said the falcon.

Alex clambered onto the great bird's back and managed to bury himself in a mass of soft feathers. Orion's Messenger took off in a rush of cold air and Alex felt a thrill as they climbed higher and higher into the night sky. He glanced back only once, just long enough to see the twinkling streetlights fade as they disappeared into the darkness.

They had been flying for many hours when Alex peered out over the falcon's graceful wings. Even in the grey light of dawn he could see it was going to be a beautiful day, for there was not a cloud in the sky. Alex looked around with growing curiosity. Orion's Messenger was flying lower as they approached a small island surrounded by crystal clear blue waters with waves gently lapping against the soft yellow sand on the shore.

"Why does it all look so familiar?" Alex was puzzled as he thought for a moment. "Of course, I know! The place I imagined when I was up in the loft yesterday. How amazing! It is real after all!"

He asked Orion's Messenger if this is where they were heading to.

"It is indeed and it is called 'Blue Sky Island'," said the falcon.

Alex sat up, more awake now. He gazed around with interest as they flew over some gently rolling hills in many different shades of green. They passed a patchwork of fields in a blaze of gold, where the crops of barley and corn were ready for harvesting. By the edge of the fields, Alex saw a cluster of freshly painted little houses, with neat colourful gardens.

"What a nice place. I wonder who lives there," he thought and, close by, he noticed a cobbled village square with a grand old clock tower.

Continuing their journey, Orion's Messenger flew over to the other side of the island. Alex was shocked to see how different the landscape was. The earth became cracked and a dusty brown in colour and the fields all around were stark and bare. They flew over a wood filled with half-dead trees – not a leaf to be seen on any of the withered tree branches. Also, a stream that should have been brimming with pure, clear water, was instead filled with murky brown sludge that was chugging along over stony pebbles.

A short distance from the stream, Alex spotted a group of dingy huts that looked dirty and run down. Whoever was living there didn't care a hoot because the place was a complete mess. Heaps of rubbish were scattered about, and the smoke rising from an open bonfire left a rather nasty smell in the air.

"Everything looks so dreadful here, I wonder why it's all so bad on this side of the island," thought Alex.

He was very relieved when Orion's Messenger left that horrible place behind and before long they were flying over the Rolling Green Hills once more. Lower and lower as his strong wings flapped, Orion's Messenger finally came to a halt on the grass outside a pretty white cottage.

Alex was stiff from holding on for such a long time. He clambered down awkwardly from the great bird and straightened himself up.

"What do I do now?" he asked the falcon.

"Knock on that front door and say I brought you here," said Orion's Messenger, "I have delivered you safely and now I must leave. We shall meet again sooner than you think."

Before Alex had a chance to say another word, Orion's Messenger took to the air and was gone in an instant. Alex stood alone on the grass and wondered what on earth was going to happen next.

Chapter 5.
Making New Friends

Alex looked at the small cottage in front of him. It was quite old fashioned with diamond-shaped windows and a bright yellow front door. The roof was thatched and on top of the roof was a weathervane in the shape of a cockerel which was pointing in a southerly direction. He noticed white puffs of smoke curling out of the chimney pot and then he read the sign above the front door, 'Welcome to Country Cottage'. Strange and colourful flowers filled the garden, the likes of which he had never seen before. Some were like purple lollipops, the size of dinner plates. Others were like huge rainbow-striped butterflies fluttering in the breeze. The sun was shining brightly and a sonata songbird chirped in a peach tree nearby.

Alex approached the front door and took the silvery star-shaped knocker in his hand. He hesitated for a moment before knocking gently, 'knock, knock'. No one came to the door. He knocked again, only this time much louder, 'KNOCK, KNOCK, KNOCK'. Still no reply. Alex bent down and pushed open the letter box. Peering inside he saw a cluttered kitchen, with a copper kettle sitting on an old-fashioned iron stove. An empty rocking chair full of worn cushions was leaning up against a bookcase crammed with dusty old books. In the middle of the room he saw a table spread with the delights of a breakfast that had not yet been eaten. It made Alex realise how hungry he was.

Suddenly, Alex had a feeling that he was being watched. He was quite right, for there, sitting on the garden path behind him, was a large white cat, who was observing him through big emerald green eyes. Alex turned around and noticed that the cat had a black tail and one of its ears was also black. He was not at all surprised when the cat spoke to him.

"There's no point in knocking on the door because he is in the back garden," said the cat.

"Excuse me," said Alex, "But *who* exactly is *he?*"

The cat looked puzzled. "Well, you *are* knocking on the front door of Ordompom the Wizard, so it is plain to me, that it is *he* whom you've come to see."

"Did you say Ordom-dom the Wizard?" queried Alex.

"Or-Dom-Pom!" said the cat sharply.

"I'm sorry, a wizard by the name of Ordompom lives here, you say?"

"Exactly, and I am Pusspom, the Wizard's best friend," said the cat.

At that moment, Alex noticed a red squirrel with a bushy tail scampering along the fence. "I am the Wizard's best friend too. I *am* the Wizard's best friend and my name is Reema," piped the squirrel indignantly, "Don't listen to her. She thinks she's the cat's whiskers!"

Alex chuckled at these two creatures. In a different world he would have been shocked to hear animals talking. However, since his flight with Orion's Messenger he understood that anything magical could happen now.

"Good morning, Pusspom. And good morning, Reema. My name is Alex and I would like to meet Ordompom. Please take me to him."

"This way," said Pusspom.

Alex followed the fluffy cat through the side gate and into the back garden, with Reema bobbing along beside them. In the far corner of the garden Alex spotted an old man with a slight stoop. He was wearing a blue and white check shirt with rolled-up sleeves. His dark green baggy trousers were held in place by red braces, with silvery stars studded all over them. Salt and pepper coloured hair curled over the back of his collar and he had a flowing white beard, just like you'd expect a wizard to have. Also, he was wearing some gold-rimmed half spectacles, which were perched right on the end of his nose. Alex watched as the wizard had a tug-of-war with a weed that didn't want to come out of the flower bed. Alex stepped forward and spoke to him.

"Er, hello, Mr Ordompom," he said sounding a bit unsure of himself.

Ordompom turned around and peered at him through his half glasses.

"And who might you be?" he queried.

"My name is Alex. Orion's Messenger brought me here," said Alex, a little nervously.

"Say that again," said Ordompom, as if he hadn't heard correctly.

"I'm Alex. I flew here with Orion's Messenger."

"That's what I thought you said!" exclaimed the Wizard and, to Alex's amazement, the old man whooped with delight, shouting, "Hooray! The magic finally worked, hooray!"

The Wizard could barely contain his excitement as he beamed at Alex.

"Well, well, well, the messenger found you at last! Now then, you must be very tired after such a long journey. Do come and join us for some breakfast."

Alex walked back to the cottage with Ordompom. Once inside, he found the place even more cluttered than he'd seen through the letterbox. For sitting on the kitchen shelves was an assortment of coloured glass bottles filled with magic potions and beside them, some weird-looking lumps of sparkly rock were fixed to the wall.

"What an odd collection," thought Alex.

Then his eyes rested on the table in the middle of the kitchen. Warm, crusty rolls were placed on a bread board. Round jars of homemade apricot and strawberry jam sat next to a glass jug brimming with golden apple juice. There was a selection of cheeses on a large blue plate, surrounded by little pots of fruity yoghurt and a bowl piled high with bright red cherries. What a heavenly sight to see!

As Ordompom made himself a cup of tea, he invited Alex to sit down beside him.

"Tuck in, Alex, and do try some of my freshly baked rolls and delicious strawberry jam," he said, pushing a tempting pot towards him.

Alex took one of the crusty rolls and spread it thickly with jam. He sank his teeth in and the taste was indeed delicious! He quickly polished off another roll, just like that, and followed it with a handful of the juiciest cherries he'd ever eaten. Then he drank a glassful of the golden apple juice. Nobody spoke much at the table whilst this jolly hearty breakfast was being eaten. But once Ordompom had poured his second cup of tea, he went over to his old rocking chair, sat down in it and gently rocked back and forth. Alex was wiping off his sticky fingers and waited patiently to hear what the Wizard had to say.

Chapter 6.
Once Upon A Time...

Ordompom took a sip from his cup of tea and began to tell his tale.

"This story begins a long, long time ago, when my greatest grandfather 'Ord the Great' walked down from the sky on the Staircase of Stars. He needed somewhere to live and so he created Blue Sky Island. It was the kind of place only wizards or magicians can conjure up and it was perfect for his every need. He had a pleasant cottage to live in, with warm sunshine all the year round and lots of peace and quiet to create new magic spells. He lived quite contentedly on his own through many changing seasons but, as time went by, Ord the Great longed for some company. He invited friends from above the Staircase of Stars to come and stay with him on the island. It wasn't long before little white cottages started popping up here and there and a village was created. Everyone settled in well, living in peace and harmony in their new-found homes. There was no need for words like 'nasty,' 'horrible,' or 'evil,' because those kinds of things just didn't happen on Blue Sky Island.

Season after season unfolded and, as Ord the Great grew old, he knew that one day soon he would have to return to the 'Elder Wizard's Rest Home' in the sky. He also knew that the people of the island would need protecting once he was gone. He thought about it long and hard and decided to leave the islanders a legacy. On his very last day on Blue Sky Island, he called all the people to a meeting in the cobbled main square and gathered everyone around him. In front of them all, he turned a piece of solid gold into a magnificent Golden Eagle.

'I name this eagle "Orion",' he said with a flourish of his magic wand, 'Whilst he lives and breathes on this island, you shall be safe.' Then he waved his magic wand in the air once more and, from nowhere, appeared a sparkling round object, no bigger than a tennis ball. It bobbed around and glittered in mid-air. Ord took the magical thingamajig and cupped it in his hands.

'This,' he announced grandly, 'is the Magic Orb.'

He showed it to the people of the island and they gazed at it with fascination. 'The Magic Orb will remain with you and help to guard against any danger that could befall you. But I have one condition to make. Every year, at the same time, Orion must bring the Magic Orb to the Elder Wizard's Rest Home in the sky. The powerful force of the Orb will then be renewed and strengthened to protect Blue Sky Island and all the islanders. If, on any occasion, Orion does not return to the Staircase of Stars, then I cannot say what will happen.' Ord the Great looked at them very seriously, 'Please make sure that Orion and the Magic Orb make the journey every year as instructed.'

With that, he placed the Magic Orb in Orion's talons and faced the islanders. 'Goodbye, dear friends. I shall miss you all.' And in a puff of smoke he disappeared.

The islanders now turned their gaze to Orion – such a magnificent Golden Eagle with glittering ruby eyes.

Orion knew he had come to protect the people of Blue Sky Island. And so, with his great wings soaring in the breeze, he firmly grasped the Magic Orb and headed off in the direction of the Rolling Green Hills. He sought out the Lime Leaf Acacia Trees where he decided to make his new home.

Well Alex, all that happened many, many moons ago. Now I will tell you what happened recently," sighed Ordompom, as he continued his story.

"It was the time of the year for Orion to return to the Elder Wizard's Rest Home once again. I watched him fly away with the Magic Orb. As always, it was a wonderful sight to see him gliding through the air, but then suddenly, from nowhere, a great gust of wind blew the Magic Orb right out of Orion's talons! The Magic Orb must have landed somewhere to the north of the Rolling Green Hills. Orion searched desperately, but he couldn't find it anywhere. So, he came back to the village for help. We were all surprised to see him back again so soon, and without the Magic Orb too. He seemed to be overcome with extreme tiredness and landed on top of the Many-a-Moon Clock Tower in the village square. Everyone thought he'd stopped for a rest, but he hasn't moved since. He's stuck there, perched alongside Mr Many-a-Moon and frozen in time."

Ordompom looked into his empty teacup and decided to refill it. He sat down and looked glumly at Alex, "Since then, things have started to go horribly wrong."

Alex had been listening closely to Ordompom. "Whatever has happened?" he asked with concern.

"Well Alex, because the protective powers of the Magic Orb were not renewed, it didn't take long for an intruder to arrive on the island. The unwelcome visitor

is a monstrous giant of an ogre who calls himself, 'The Grizzly Grumpot'. He is evil and quite frightening to behold as he is indeed an enormous fellow. Not a single hair does he have on the top of his head, yet his eyebrows are bushy and he has a chin full of bristly black whiskers. His eyes have a dark and mean look about them. When the wind is in the right direction, his voice can be heard from the other side of the island, bellowing orders and instructions to the rotten gang he brought with him, and they are called the 'Grim-Groms'. Very strange creatures they are too, so short and round of stature with bright orange eyes and ears that are pointed and yellow like baby corns. On top of their heads they have one curl, just like a piglet's tail. They rock from side to side as they walk with duck-like webbed feet. Oh, and by the way, they are extremely green in colour!

It is ten moons past since they landed on the north side of the island, in a fleet of poddy paddle boats. Those horrid fellows invaded the Yellowood Woods, where we have our finest and most ancient of trees. They have been living there ever since and it is dreadful how they are ruining the place! Before The Grizzly Grumpot and the Grim-Groms set up camp, everything was fresh, green and alive, just as it is here. Alex, you must have seen the contrast when you flew over our beautiful Island."

Alex had to agree. Things did look pretty grim on the other side of the island and he was upset to hear such a sorry tale.

"Ordompom, you are a wizard. Surely you can do something to get rid of The Grizzly Grumpot and the Grim-Groms?"

"Oh Alex, if only I could, but I do have an unusual problem. You see I'm a 'Midi-Magician'," said Ordompom.

"What do you mean?" asked Alex, curiously.

"Well, it's like this. I was never blessed with a great talent for spell making, try as I might to practise and improve. As the years have gone by, it has become more difficult for me, and my spells only work now and then except for the simplest ones of all. See how long it took for Orion's Messenger to bring you here. If I were a better wizard, you would have arrived much sooner." The Wizard shook his head with regret.

"Well, I'm here now so your magic did work Ordompom," said Alex, trying to cheer him up. "And by the way, why did you choose me?"

The Wizard looked over the top of his half glasses and beckoned him to come closer. "There is something very special about you Alex. You may not know it, but you have a 'magical dezora' around you."

"What *ever* is that?" blurted out Alex.

"It's something you can't see, something you can't feel, something you can't even smell or touch," said the Wizard seriously.

"I don't understand. What's the point?"

"The 'magical dezora' radiates invisible positive vibes. It stops harm from coming your way and enables you to ward off the Grottynots."

"Ward off the Grottynots?" Alex looked very puzzled.

"Oh yes," beamed Ordompom, "You know – changing beastly and gruesome into something good, or reversing doom and gloom for something nice and pleasant. That kind of thing."

At this point Alex was wide-eyed with amazement. This was the stuff that story books were made of! "Could it be true that I'm wearing an invisible shield and I don't even know it – what excitement!" he thought to himself.

"I'll help in any way I can," offered Alex, "But firstly tell me more about The Grizzly Grumpot."

Ordompom carried on telling his tale. "A dark shadow has been cast over Blue Sky Island since the arrival of The Grizzly Grumpot and he takes great delight in disrupting our lives with his destructive ways. Getting up to terrible mischief, we don't know what he will do next. The other day he was messing around with the weather and we had Rainshine Moonbow for the second time in a week."

"Cripes! What's Rainshine Moonbow?" exclaimed Alex.

"Hah! It starts off with rain and sunshine together, which makes a wonderful rainbow. It's so lovely to see an arc of many colours in the sky... but then, he might turn day into night, which is dreadfully confusing and the weather becomes worse, with the rain changing to hailstones the size of gobstoppers! Alex, we have to find a way to halt this soon, as the islanders are fearful that so much rain will flood our fields and ruin all our crops!"

"How awful, this is all just too bad!" gulped Alex.

"These goings on are only affecting this side of the island. No bad weather is happening around the Yellowood Woods where The Grizzly Grumpot has his encampment. If anything, it's dreadfully dry and dusty over there."

"I must say, it does look terribly parched and bleak," agreed Alex.

"There's even more to this story. Some of the villagers have gone missing and we don't know what has happened to them. The Grizzly Grumpot *must* have something to do with their disappearance. And, as for the Grim-Groms, they have become such a nuisance in our lives. They skulk into the village after dark and tip over our dustbins, scavenging through the rotting contents, grunting and screeching and making so much noise fighting over the mouldy scraps they love to eat. Rubbish is scattered in a messy trail as they leave the village."

Ordompom let out a sorrowful sigh and continued, "Also, they frighten the poor cows in the local barns, so they're not producing half the milk they used to."

"Oh my goodness, no wonder you're upset Ordompom," said Alex.

"The Grizzly Grumpot would *love* to get his hands on the Magic Orb. If he did, it would be a complete disaster for all the good people living here and life on Blue Sky Island would never be the same again," groaned Ordompom.

"Then we have to find the Magic Orb before The Grizzly Grumpot does," said Alex with determination.

"You're quite right. That's exactly what we have to do. In fact, we're very lucky The Grizzly Grumpot hasn't

41

found it already. So we have no time to lose!" answered Ordompom.

"Where do we start?" asked Alex eagerly.

"Well Alex, I'm going to search through my *Midi-Magician's Best Spell Book*. I'll find the right spell to cast over you and, with a bit of luck, you'll lead us to the Magic Orb."

"I can't believe it's that simple to do," said Alex.

"My powers are at their strongest in the middle of the night and that's when the spells work best. If you remember Alex, that is the time when Orion's Messenger came to collect you and brought you here."

With that, he heaved himself slowly out of his rocking chair and went over to the crammed bookcase. Adjusting his spectacles, he peered at the worn old books in front of him and ran his finger along the shelf until he found what he was looking for.

Then he muttered under his breath, "Hmmm ah yes, here we are."

He pulled out an ancient leather-bound volume filled with handwritten spells and strange mystical drawings that were fading with age.

Ordompom blew the dust off it as a small spider scuttled across the front of his treasured book. He carefully turned over the brittle pages one at a time and eventually he said, "Ah ha! This is just what I'm looking for – 'The Seek and Find Spell'."

Carefully, he placed a blackbird feather between the pages as a bookmark, and he turned to Alex, "Tonight, we'll see what happens. But there's nothing more to be done now, so I suggest you go into the village with Pusspom and Reema. They will show you where poor

Orion is stranded on top of the Many-a-Moon Clock Tower."

Pusspom meowed as she appeared from under the table.

"I will show you how to get there Alex. Follow me."

"Don't follow that cat! I know a better way, a better way!" piped Reema. He was bobbing about in earnest trying to catch Alex's attention.

"Come along now, there's enough trouble brewing as it is. You can *both* show Alex the way. Be off with you and let me get back to my gardening! Now, where did I put my rose cutters?" he muttered to himself, as he walked out of the back door.

Chapter 7.

Alex Looks Up And
Up And Up

Alex followed Pusspom and Reema as they strolled along Linden Lane towards the village. It was mid-morning and some of the islanders were out and about. He saw one little old lady sweeping her garden path and she leant on her broom to watch them go by. He nodded to her and Pusspom said, "That's Miss Petranella and she's 101 years old! Sometimes she lets me sleep on her sunny porch." She purred with pleasure. Further along the lane they passed a teenage boy perched up a ladder. He was picking lots of wild blackberries and dropping them one at a time into a large wicker basket.

"Hello Hamilton. What are you going to do with all those blackberries?" asked Pusspom.

"I'm collecting them for Mrs Meredith. She's going to make some jam to sell in the village square," replied Hamilton. Alex smiled at the thought of all that scrumptious jam!

Then Alex heard some young children playing in a garden nearby. They peered over the hedge with curiosity, never having seen Alex before, and asked if he'd throw back their ball, which was sitting on the path. He smiled at them, picked up the ball and threw it over the hedge.

The end of the lane opened up into the village square where a farmer's market was taking place. Alex surveyed the bustling scene in front of him. The islanders were busy buying fruit and vegetables from Mr Timifig the greengrocer, and they were haggling over the price of his carrots and freshly picked peas. On the next stall, Bellabree the cheese lady was selling a variety of cow, sheep and goats' cheeses. She offered Alex a morsel of goats' cheese to try, but he found the taste a bit too strong for his liking.

Mr Frimisto the fishmonger was busy displaying his sardines, herrings and other fish straight from the sea around Blue Sky Island. He waved at Alex to buy some of his smoked haddock, but Alex politely said, "No thank you."

They continued walking on the cobblestones through the market and, as they strolled past a stall with necklaces, bracelets and other girlie stuff, Alex suddenly stopped in his tracks. For selling those bits and bobs was Miss Candy Pink!

"Whatever are you doing here?" he said, his voice full of surprise.

"Oh, hello Alex. This is my home and I spend most of my time on Blue Sky Island. However, Orion's Messenger flies me over to work in the museum every other week, which is what I love to do too," she beamed. Alex couldn't believe what he was hearing or what he was seeing. For here was Miss Candy Pink, living proof that someone could actually live between two worlds. How amazing was that?!

Miss Candy Pink turned to Alex. "I sensed your magical dezora when you bought that special poster in the museum recently and I knew you were 'The One'.

I was sure then that we'd meet again soon." She gave him her biggest smile and, without any further explanation, she turned to help another customer.

Alex stood and stared at her for a moment, but then he walked on with Pusspom and Reema until they reached the other side of the square where they finally ground to a halt and Pusspom turned to Alex.

"We've arrived. This is the Many-a-Moon Clock Tower," and she pointed towards it with her paw.

Alex looked at the tall old building in front of him, which went up and up and up. At the very top of the tower was a four-sided clock with a white face surrounded by big black numbers. Above the clock and on each of the four corners of the tower, Mr. Many-a-Moon smiled down on the village square. When the clock struck on the hour, chiming bells would ring out, and the tower was so high, that the clock could be seen for miles around.

"There is our dear Protector Orion," said Pusspom.

Squinting in the sunlight, Alex could just see Orion perched on the top of the tower. The Golden Eagle did not look splendid or magnificent, as Ordompom had described him. At this moment he looked all alone, very sad and completely out of reach.

"We have to rescue Orion, don't we Alex?" piped Reema.

"We most certainly do," said Alex firmly, as he tried to imagine the day when Orion would fly away from his lonely perch.

They stayed for a while and wandered around by The Clock Tower, constantly looking up. Before leaving, Alex and the others gave Orion a friendly wave, as they knew he was watching them. Then they wandered back through the village square, where there was less hustle and bustle. Lots of goods had been sold and the traders were packing up the rest of their wares. Pusspom sidled up to Alex.

"I really need to get back to the house as I've missed my usual catnap in the warm sunshine," she purred.

The time had slipped by and the three of them made their way back to Country Cottage, where Ordompom was already busy preparing supper.

"Alex, did you manage to see Orion?" asked the Wizard, as he stood over the stove stirring a big pot of tomato soup.

Alex nodded, "Yes I did. He looked so forlorn on top of the Many-a-Moon Clock Tower, stuck and unable to move."

"Well, we'll try our best to find the Magic Orb tonight. Now then, who would like some of my delicious soup?" said Ordompom briskly.

"Yes please, I love tomato soup," said Alex earnestly.

Ordompom dug into the tureen with his large soup ladle and handed Alex a steaming bowlful. Then he said, "After we've eaten, we'll head up to bed to snatch a few hours' sleep. We have a long night ahead of us."

As light faded, Alex found himself climbing the narrow rickety staircase to the spare bedroom. He bent his head low to enter the tiny room. He was very tired after his first day on Blue Sky Island. He crawled into the soft downy bed, falling asleep the minute his head touched the pillow.

After what seemed no time at all Alex was awoken by a sharp tugging of his bedcover. It was Reema's way of telling him to get up and Alex had to stop and think where he was for a moment. He rubbed his eyes and listened for, in the distance, he could hear midnight striking in the Many-a-Moon Clock Tower and melodious chimes rang out. He got dressed quickly and went down to the kitchen. Ordompom was standing there in his official wizard's clothes. He was wearing a long, black flowing robe covered in stars and his pointed hat was a glossy black with glitter sprinkled all over it. In one hand he held the most precious item a wizard can have – a mystical magic wand – and under his arm was tucked the *Midi-Magician's Best Spell Book*. He looked quite splendid. Peering out from under his robe was Pusspom and she had a glow-in-the-dark collar around her neck. As for Reema, he was busy scampering about, excited at what was about to happen.

Ordompom led them all outside. It was a lovely clear night and the light from the moon was so bright it lit up the garden. Alex gazed up at the stars in the deep blue velvet sky and he was amazed at how brilliantly they sparkled.

"You can look at the stars another evening, we have important work to do now," advised Ordompom.

"It's such a wonderful sight," sighed Alex and he continued to admire the stars for a little longer.

"Now then, come into the centre of the garden and stand here by the sundial. I want you to look into Pusspom's eyes," commanded Ordompom.

Alex saw a pair of big emerald green cat's eyes staring right at him in the darkness and he was mesmerised. Ordompom walked in a circle around Alex, waving his mystical magic wand and chanting as he went:

"NO ONE KNOWS WHERE YOU MAY GO,
BUT IF YOU CAN THE WAY YOU'LL SHOW,
WE'LL FOLLOW YOU UNTIL YOU STOP,
PLEASE LEAD US TO THE VERY SPOT.
SEEK AND FIND THE MAGIC ORB,
SEEK AND FIND IT NOW."

Ordompom kept repeating the magic words but nothing happened. So, after a while, Alex said, "Um, Ordompom, I don't think your spell is working."

"Oh fiddlesticks! If that is so, then I shall have to go back into the house and consult with the Galactic Rocks," exclaimed Ordompom, as he stroked his beard, "Hmmm yes, I think that's what I'll do."

"Whatever is he talking about?" whispered Alex to Pusspom.

"Remember all those strange lumps of rock hanging on the wall in the kitchen? Well, when Ordompom looks at them, he sees many strange and enchanted things deep within them. That's what helps him to make decisions," said Pusspom.

"I've never heard of such a thing," replied Alex.

"They were part of the legacy from Ord the Great, when he came down on the Staircase of Stars," continued Pusspom, "And those rocks have been very helpful to Ordompom in the past."

Ordompom shrugged his shoulders and gave a disappointed sigh. Finally, he started to walk back up the garden path muttering aloud, "Time to consult with the Galactic Rocks, yes I think I'll do that."

He wasn't too surprised that the spell hadn't worked for, after all, he was only a Midi-Magician. But hold on a minute... just as he was about to enter the cottage he felt a hand pulling at his sleeve. It was Alex looking at him in a most strange way.

"What is it Alex?" asked Ordompom. Alex said nothing but beckoned him to follow.

"Pusspom! Reema! The spell - I think it *is* working after all. Quickly, let's follow Alex!" shouted Ordompom excitedly.

With no time to spare, they went after Alex as he walked briskly down the path towards Linden Lane and across the village square. They were soon out of the village and approaching the first field of the Rolling Green Hills. Alex hoisted himself up and over a five-bar gate in an instant.

Ordompom looked dismayed. He rattled the gate to see if would open, but no such luck — it was padlocked.

"Hey, slow down Alex, my old bones can't move so quickly!" shouted the Wizard, as he struggled to clamber over the gate. Alex didn't hear him and pressed steadily on. Suddenly it dawned on Ordompom that Alex was heading for the Yellowood Woods.

"Oh drat the bat! I do hope he's not going into the woods. We don't want to bump into The Grizzly Grumpot!" exclaimed Ordompom.

Unfortunately for them, Alex did not stop. He went through a field of barley and then the terrain changed to hard, dry ground as they followed him. Ordompom knew they were now very close to the woods and he became more alarmed with each footstep. But there was no holding back as Alex started to weave his way in and out of the tall bare trees. It was dark and creepy in there and they were surrounded by the noises of the night. Owls hooting, wolves howling and rustling sounds close by, as who-knows-what scurried by. Pusspom and Reema did not like that scary place at all and they kept looking behind them as they moved quietly along.

Finally, Alex ground to a halt right beside the tallest Yellowood tree of all, which also happened to be the oldest tree in the woods. He stood by its gnarled and twisted branches and then he did something most peculiar. He started to jump on the spot.

Ordompom was so exhausted and out of breath from the long and difficult trek. But he managed to watch Alex jumping up and down.

"What is he doing?" said Pusspom.

Ordompom straightened his glasses and wiped his brow.

"My guess is that the Magic Orb must have fallen down somewhere around here," he pointed towards the tree.

"But, but … we can't search now, it's much too dark!" piped Reema nervously.

"I fear you're quite right Reema," puffed the Wizard, for he was still out of breath, "However, now we know where to come, we'll take our chances and return tomorrow in the daytime to look for the Magic Orb." Ordompom was still puffing as he peered into the darkness and listened hard just in case there were any uninvited guests lurking around. Nothing aroused his suspicion, but still he whispered, "I think we should leave as quickly as possible."

And with that, Ordompom stuck a dead branch in the ground next to the tree, marking the very spot where they needed to return to. Then he commanded Alex to 'turnabout' and the four of them rapidly left the woods and headed for home.

Chapter 8.
A Sack Full Of Sparrow Feathers

Unknown to Alex, Ordompom, Pusspom and Reema, they had been spotted from the very first moment they arrived in the woods. It was just their bad luck that Joscal and Tilano, the most horrid members of the Grizzly Grumpot's Gang, were guarding the camp that very evening. They were the worst kind of Grim-Grom you could ever have the misfortune to meet. Cranky and quarrelsome, Joscal was easy to recognise because his eyes were bright turquoise, not orange like all the other Grim-Groms. Also he enjoyed whinging for no good reason. Tilano, on the other hand, was the largest roly-poly Grim-Grom of all. He waddled about with his green hands on his hips. He was sullen and sly and, when he spoke, he sounded just like a dog barking.

Joscal and Tilano nodded to one another in silence as they watched Ordompom and the others leaving the Yellowood Woods. Then they made their way to the Grizzly Grumpot's hut as fast as their little waddly feet could carry them. Through the dreary cluster of mud huts they made their way and, even though it was a clear, dry evening, the air smelt musty and damp around the campsite.

Most of the Grim-Groms were fast asleep and there was no sound to be heard when they knocked upon the Grizzly Grumpot's door. He must have been sleeping too, for it took a while before they heard a tired voice growling from within, "Who knocks so late?"

"It is Joscal and Tilano with important news for you, Your Great Grumpiness."

They heard The Grizzly Grumpot grumbling under his breath as he came shuffling towards the door.

"I suppose you'd better come in," he snorted, as he pulled open the rickety, creaking door. The two Grim-Groms waddled into the room. Lying on the dirty floor was an enormous brown sack stuffed with sparrow feathers, hedgehog quills and hay, which The Grizzly Grumpot was using as a makeshift bed. In the corner of the room stood a large yellow candle on an upturned crate. Its flame gave the room an eerie light and cast flickering shadows on the wall. The candle was melting slowly and dripping wax onto the crate below. There were cobwebs everywhere and a couple of large rats scurried out through the open door.

The Grizzly Grumpot beckoned the two Grim-Groms to step inside the hut. Standing there and yawning sleepily, he scratched the back of his head as he listened to Joscal and Tilano tell their story. Then he let out a loud vile grunt when he heard that Alex seemed to have found the very spot where the Magic Orb lay.

The Grizzly Grumpot grunted again with satisfaction. "Now I know why you two are my best guards. You have done well. We will grab that Orby thing from under their noses and I shall become the Master of Bloo Sky Island!" He rubbed his hands together with glee.

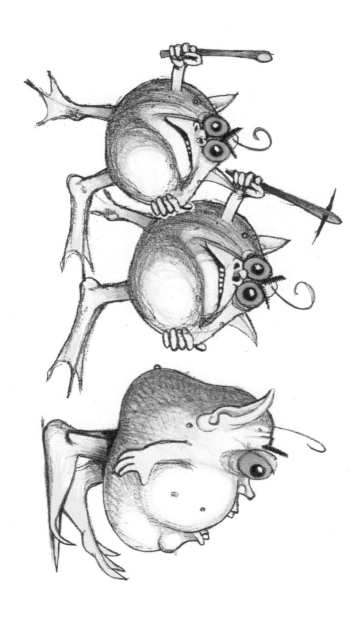

"Does that mean we need not roam the high seas anymore?" barked Tilano.

"And can we stay here forever?" whinged Joscal.

"This place will be ours!" exclaimed The Grizzly Grumpot shaking his fist in triumph.

If you had seen what happened next, you would not have believed it, as in the very next moment, Joscal and Tilano promptly burst into tears!! Now you have to understand the strange behaviour of the Grim-Groms. For the happier they are, the sadder they appear to be. So, it wasn't at all surprising for The Grizzly Grumpot to see both Joscal and Tilano standing there, with tears rolling down their round green faces!

"Off you go and get back to your guard duty," commanded The Grizzly Grumpot. He let the wailing pair out of his hut, "And now perhaps I can get some rest!"

Well, those two nasty Grim-Groms were so miserably overjoyed that they decided to wake up the rest of the camp and tell them the good news. Soon everyone was awake, and the weird sound of Grim-Groms blubbering with unhappy happiness filled the air. The Grizzly Grumpot was livid at being disturbed again. He nearly wrenched the hut door off its hinges, as he stuck his head out and roared,

"Be quiet, the lot of you! I'm trying to get some sleep!!"

Chapter 9.
Back To The Woods

The following morning a gentle ray of sunlight eased its way through the early morning mist. Ordompom stretched lazily and gazed out of his bedroom window as he recalled last night's adventure.

"Mr Midi-Magician, my foot! It's nice to know that my spells *really* can work," he thought. He heard Pusspom meowing outside his door.

"Just coming," he called, and Pusspom followed him down to the kitchen for a saucer of milk.

Reema was snuggled up in his favourite hidey-hole on top of the old bookcase waiting for something to eat. Ordompom put out a handful of hazelnuts for him.

Alex appeared at the kitchen door wearing a snugly green dressing gown borrowed from Ordompom. The large dressing gown trailed on the floor and, because the sleeves were far too long, they hid his hands too.

"Why am I so tired? I feel like I've been up half the night," he mumbled.

"Oh, but you have!" chuckled Ordompom.

"What are you talking about?" asked Alex in a puzzled voice.

Ordompom retold the events of the previous evening and described how Alex had led them in a great hurry to the oldest tree in the Yellowood Woods. Alex listened in complete amazement.

"Golly, gosh! I don't remember anything at all. Not the trek across the fields or going into the woods. And I certainly don't remember jumping up and down on the spot. Why, I can't even recall climbing into bed when we got back to the cottage."

"You certainly showed us the way last night, and today we will return to the Yellowood Woods even though it's very risky to go back in broad daylight. We know just where to look, so we'll take great care and, with a bit of luck, we *shall* find the Magic Orb!" beamed Ordompom.

With that, Ordompom went to the stove and got busy toasting some crumpets for Alex and himself. Breakfast was soon demolished and Alex rushed upstairs to change clothes, nearly tripping over the trailing dressing gown as he went. It wasn't long before they all gathered at the back door raring to go.

"Right then, let's be on our way," said Ordompom, and the four of them left the cottage, tumbling down Linden Lane and across the village square. As they arrived at the first field by the Rolling Green Hills, everyone waited patiently whilst Ordompom slowly hoisted himself up and over that wretched five-bar gate again. Eventually they came close to the Yellowood Woods and Ordompom turned to Alex, Pusspom and Reema. He raised his forefinger to his lips, "Shhhh. We must be ever so quiet and move very carefully while we're in the woods. You never know where a Grim-Grom might be hiding."

And so, the little group slowly weaved their way through the trees, trying not to make any noise and doing their best not to be seen.

They were blissfully unaware that their every move was being watched by lots of hidden orange eyes – in the sparse bushes and behind the forlorn trees, from a distance and close by too. Unfortunately for them, the Grim-Groms were everywhere and silently looking on.

Soon, Ordompom and the others were standing by the oldest tree in the woods once more. They pulled the dead branch out of the ground that marked the spot where Alex had jumped up and down. The Wizard walked around the tree and appeared to be deep in thought as he stroked his beard. He said in a whisper,

"Many moons past, when Orion flew away, I did wonder where he dropped the Magic Orb. So now I ask myself the very question, 'Where did it go?' Maybe it landed up in the tree branches, or maybe down on the ground and it is hidden under some dead leaves." Ordompom pointed up in the air and then he pointed down and beckoned Reema the squirrel to come closer. He spoke to him in a soft voice.

"Reema, I want you to scoot up to the top of the tree and see if you can spot anything small and glittery there. Take a jolly good look and, whilst you're doing that, we'll have a scout around down here."

The red squirrel nodded to Ordompom and scuttled up the tree, his tail waving like a fluffy flag behind him as he went. Down below, Alex swept back the carpet of dried leaves from the tree trunk and went on his hands and knees to take a look. Pusspom scrabbled at the earth with her dainty paws and Ordompom sifted through some dead leaves trying to find the precious object. Up and above them they could hear Reema scurrying about, when suddenly he gave a squeal of excitement.

"Shhh, not so loud Reema, what's all the fuss about?" Ordompom said in a husky whisper.

"Well I'm not sure, but I think there's something up here in an abandoned nest. I'm going to take a closer look," replied Reema.

Everyone stopped what they were doing. There was a hushed silence as they waited for what seemed an awfully long time, whilst Reema scampered along a high branch in the tree to inspect his find.

"I think it must be the Magic Orb! Would you like me to tip over the old nest and see what drops out of it?" he piped with excitement.

"Yes, yes go ahead and do that," said Ordompom.

All eyes were on Reema and a rustling noise could be heard as he pushed the nest over. Within moments a small dazzling light came plummeting towards them.

"Here it comes!" said Alex in a loud whisper. He tried to catch the object, but it shot straight through his hands and landed with a soft 'plop' on the leafy ground. The 'thing' sat there sparkling all the colours of the rainbow. Gathering around, they stared at it with fascination.

Ordompom bent down and picked it up, gently turning it over in his hands.

"Tickle a toad and dance with a dingo, this is most splendid! Well done Reema, you *have* found the Magic Orb!!" he exclaimed and smiled with delight as the squirrel came scurrying back down the tree.

"I've never seen anything quite like it before," said Alex in a hushed tone, "And I can feel its magical power."

"Meow, it's purrrfectly beautiful," purred Pusspom.

"This is great news and it means that we can finally get rid of the Grizzly Grumpot. Soon, all our troubles will be over!" sighed Ordompom with relief.

"THAT'S WHAT YOU THINK!" A deafening voice boomed out from behind and made them all nearly jump out of their skins. So engrossed had they been in their search, that not one of them had heard the Grizzly Grumpot and his gang creeping up on them. Now they were completely surrounded!

The Grizzly Grumpot took a menacing step forward.

"That sparkly thing you're holdin' — I'll take it," he growled, "Come on, hand it over."

Ordompom held the Magic Orb above his head and waved it defiantly. "This belongs to Orion, Protector of Blue Sky Island, and I am returning it to him immediately!"

"OH NO YOU'RE NOT! Your Protector, as you call him, is a useless bird stuck on top of an old clock tower where nobody can reach him! Bah!" roared The Grizzly Grumpot.

"He will save us from the likes of you, now that we have the Magic Orb," said Ordompom wagging his finger at him.

"Not so fast. How can he save you, when you have no way of gettin' that Orby thing to him? Give it over and be quick about it too!" snarled The Grizzly Grumpot.

Ordompom pulled the Magic Orb close to him as Alex and the others looked on with alarm. The Grizzly Grumpot strode over and snatched the Magic Orb straight out of Ordompom's hand!

"Give it back at once, d'you hear me?!" shouted Ordompom, with anger. The Grizzly Grumpot was extremely close to Ordompom and he breathed his horrible stinky breath all over him. Shocked, Ordompom took a big step back.

"Mr Has-Been Wizard! Thank you for doin' us a favour and findin' that Orby thing. I'm goin' to keep it safe 'n' sound, somewheres you can't lay your hands on it!" taunted The Grizzly Grumpot.

"The Magic Orb does not belong to you and you have no right to take it," wailed Ordompom. The Grizzly Grumpot waved the Magic Orb around.

"Well it's mine now. This little beauty is goin' to make me the Overlord of Bloo Sky Island. You lot can shove orf and don't be snoopin' around *my* side of the Island again! And if any of you *dares* to come back alookin' for that Orby thing, I shall turn you into big black cockroaches!"

He started to walk away but then he stopped in his tracks. A really mean expression came across his face and he snarled at Alex, "I think I'll turn *you* into a cockroach right now!" he pointed a big hairy finger and muttered something peculiar as he did so. Alex was alarmed, but then he remembered his 'magical dezora', so he stood quite upright as The Grizzly Grumpot continued to mutter strange words. Alex waited, but absolutely nothing happened to him.

"What's this!" came a loud bellow. The Grizzly Grumpot repeated the strange words and waved his hand around some more. Alex just stood there, larger than life. The Grizzly Grumpot was really angry and completely mystified as to why Alex hadn't changed into a big black bug.

"How dare you defy me!" he glared at Alex. "This has never happened to me before. Why haven't you turned into a cockroach you 'orrible boy you!" The Grizzly

Grumpot was desperate not to make a fool of himself so he stamped his foot down so hard that the ground shook.

"This is outrageous! Nobody interferes with the mighty might of the Grizzly Grumpot!! Be warned, all of you, Bloo Sky Island is now mine, so you stay away from my camp or else!!" he yelled, pointing another hairy finger at them and with a final gesture, he shook his fist and lumbered off with the Grim-Groms hot on his heels.

All, that is, except for Joscal and Tilano, who stood there with their hands on their roly poly green hips. They were shouting at the unhappy bunch, "The Grizzly Grumpot is going to be the Overlord of Bloo Sky Island – Nah-nah-ni-nah-nah! We're going to invite beastly folks from distant lands to come and join us. Goblins, trolls and marauding monsters, wayward witches and

flying frogbats! Yeah, the more of thems that come, the more of you's that'll be kicked orf the island! Ha-ha-ha! You'd better start packin' your bags pretty pronto cos we're stayin' for good!"

Ordompom and the others were filled with dismay as the last two Grim-Groms waddled off, yelling rude things as they went.

"Meow, this is dreadful, may your huts collapse from mud rot!" hissed Pusspom.

"Shhh, they might hear you," said Alex.

"I don't care if they do! They're a bag full of weasels!" Reema twitched his fluffy tail with annoyance.

Ordompom was shocked at what had just happened and spoke in a sad voice. "This is so disappointing. Now we are empty-handed and The Grizzly Grumpot has the Magic Orb, things are going to get much worse, I fear. I'm sorry I wasted your time by bringing you here Alex."

"All is not lost. Don't you see, my magical dezora stopped me from being turned into a cockroach, so that's a good thing isn't it?" said Alex. He tried to cheer Ordompom up and said, "Please don't send me home yet. You must make your best effort to find another spell and, with a bit of luck, we'll sort things out."

"Oh dear, if only I were a better wizard," sighed Ordompom. "I'll just have to put my thinking cap on. Or, even better, consult with the Galactic Rocks."

"Are those the strange rocks on your wall? I'd love to know more about them," asked Alex.

"I'll tell you more later, but we really need to get back to the cottage now. I don't want to spend one moment longer in this creepy place," said Ordompom forlornly.

And so, it was that the unhappy group headed for home.

Chapter 10.

A Spell That Works At Last (Well Almost)

It was mid-afternoon on the same day and Alex wandered into the kitchen where he found Ordompom facing his mysterious rocks. The Wizard was peering over his half glasses and trying to decide which one to take down off the wall. At the same time, he beckoned Alex to come closer.

"I want to tell you all about the Galactic Rocks. These are my family heirlooms which I inherited from Ord the Great. They come from a small planet called Nebilordum above the Staircase of Stars and are made from Luna Quartz. These rocks beam waves of coloured light, just like the amazing *Aurora Borealis*, which you can see in the northernmost winter night sky of your kingdom. When I hold one of these rocks in my hands, it really helps me to sort out my thoughts when I'm not sure what to do. It was one of these rocks that suggested I find you, with the aid of a magic spell of course."

Ordompom reached up and carefully took one of his precious rocks off the wall and handed it to Alex. It projected fabulous colours; the likes of which Alex had never seen before. Electric dewdrop blue, vivid sunset red, luminous waterfall green and dazzling daylight yellow. But weirdest of all were the strange whirlwind movements he could see happening deep within the rock.

"Whatever is that?" he asked.

"It's energy trapped from a bygone age and if it ever gets released – heaven only help us!!" exclaimed Ordompom.

Alex was mesmerised and wanted to spend more time holding the Luna Quartz, but Ordompom took it from him and made himself comfortable in his old chair. He sat there staring at the waves of light and then he spoke to the rock.

"I wish for some guidance please. Our beautiful island is being taken over by evil forces. Whatever are we to do?"

And so, while Ordompom focused on the Luna Quartz, Alex chatted to Reema, who was tucked in his favourite hidey-hole above the old bookcase.

"The Grizzly Grumpot really is a nasty piece of work. I wonder what he will get up to next?"

"I don't know, but my guess is that he'll be doing more of that Rainshine Moonbow with our weather – just to show everyone that *he* is now the boss," piped Reema.

"Oh deary, deary me," said Alex, glumly.

"Then we won't be able to grow anything in our vegetable patches because the ground will be too soggy. Our trees will wither away and mud and slime will affect our drinking water," said Reema, anxiously.

"If The Grizzly Grumpot believes he is the Overlord of Blue Sky Island, then surely he doesn't need to do those horrible things anymore," said Alex.

At this point, Ordompom joined in. "I think The Grizzly Grumpot will keep right on with his nasty tricks. He has to frighten us off so we don't try to rescue the Magic Orb."

"That's just too bad," said Alex.

"And now I have been advised by the Galactic Rock to cast a spell over you Alex and send you back to the Yellowood Woods again. But this time, you shall be invisible."

"Invisible? Wow! But surely there's no need for that!" exclaimed Alex.

"Well it does make sense, because then you'll be able to sneak into the Grizzly Grumpot's camp and take a close look around without him knowing. Once you discover where he is hiding the Magic Orb, you can bring it back here to safety," said Ordompom.

"That sounds like a good plan as long as the spell works well and I don't re-appear at the wrong moment!" said Alex, sounding alarmed. Then he thought about it some more and started to chuckle.

"I think it might be good fun to be invisible after all. Just imagine all the things I could get up to in the Grizzly Grumpot's camp, if nobody knows I'm there! Why, I could pick up a broom and make it float across the room before the Grizzly Grumpot's very eyes!" Alex chuckled some more.

"Your errand will be to find the Magic Orb and that's all. Now then, I will have to go through the pages of my *Midi-Magician's Best Spell Book* with great care as I've never made anyone invisible before. Indeed Alex, you will be the very first," said Ordompom seriously.

"Oh my, I wish you hadn't told me that," gasped Alex.

Ordompom got out of his chair and went over to the bookcase and pulled out his ancient book of spells.

He mulled over the pages before he found just what he was looking for.

"We'll try out this spell late tonight Alex. In the meantime, I'm going back outside to do a little more gardening. I could do with some help as my old back is creaking. So, if you'd care to join me." He put on his gardening gloves and went out of the back door.

Alex and Reema decided to follow him. By the time they got to the bottom of the garden, he was already digging hard.

"Give us a hand to plant this Hairy Fairy Moss, will you?" puffed Ordompom. Alex took a spade and they dug together in silence. Reema sat on the wooden fence, observing their every move with his big brown eyes. Suddenly, from nowhere, some dark clouds slid across the sky. Big drops of rain started to fall and Ordompom looked up as the heavens opened. He stopped what he was doing and called out, "Come on

Alex." They both dropped their spades and ran back to the cottage with Reema. Once inside, they watched as the rain poured down so hard, like buckets of water being thrown out of the sky. The torrents became huge hailstones that filled the garden and turned it into an ice-rink. Alex couldn't believe what he was seeing and Ordompom was *so* angry. He waved his fist in the air and said,

"This is all too much! Our weather is *never* this bad! The Grizzly Grumpot is up to no good again and, if this continues, I won't be able to cast my spell and send you over to The Grizzly Grumpot's camp tonight!"

"Oh dear," said Alex.

"And there's nothing we can do about it!" Ordompom shook his head with regret.

Well it rained and it hailed, and it hailed and it rained. The wind started to blow and howl around all the cracks in the windows. Chimney pots rattled, dustbins rolled over and their lids were sent flying. The heavier gusts of wind even lifted trees by their roots, causing them to topple over.

No one dared venture out in the storm and what with all that crashing and banging, nobody could sleep either! Eventually, dawn broke and, one by one, the villagers came out of their houses to inspect the damage. Their faces were filled with horror when they saw what had happened to their neatly kept gardens, which had turned into a flattened landscape of large muddy puddles. Gates and fences thrown all over the place and garden sheds destroyed, their contents lay in a tangled heap by the fury of the wind.

Ordompom looked out of his bedroom window and gave a groan. He went downstairs, pulled on his wellies and opened the back door. Without uttering a word, he splashed down the garden path and surveyed the ugly scene of mangled bushes, squashed flowers and broken tree branches. As he stood in the squelchy tip that had once been his beautiful garden, he exclaimed at the top of his voice,

"This is monstrous and beastly and I'm not putting up with it!"

He marched straight back inside and called out to Alex, Pusspom and Reema.

"There's not a moment to lose. We must stop The Grizzly Grumpot from getting up to his tricks immediately! I shall put on my wizard's robes straight away and attempt to cast a spell in bright daylight. We must find the Magic Orb as soon as possible to stop this nonsense once and for all!"

As fast as he could, Ordompom climbed the stairs and changed into his long flowing robes. He returned holding his *Midi-Magician's Best Spell Book* and peered out of the back door once again. He cast his eyes over the muddy mess in the garden and wondered if it was wise to be out there in his robes.

Stepping onto the garden path, he immediately sank into a deep puddle.

"Splish, splash, splutter! My robes are getting soaked! It's no use, I'll have to do my spell-making in the kitchen!" he exclaimed.

Back indoors, he placed the huge book on the kitchen table and beckoned to Alex.

"Come, stand here by the rocking chair and I'll try my best to make you invisible Alex. If you do disappear, talk to us and let us know you're alright." Ordompom sounded more confident than he felt, as he opened the huge dusty spell book and carefully turned over one fragile page at a time.

"Ah-ha, here we are!" he exclaimed and waved his mystical magic wand in the air.

"IN THE BRIGHTNESS OF THE DAY,
AND THE DARKNESS OF THE NIGHT,
TO MAKE SOMEBODY DISAPPEAR,
I CAST THIS SPELL WITH ALL MY MIGHT."

Ordompom repeated the spell three times. Looking up, he peered over his half glasses and was not surprised to see Alex still standing there.

"I'll keep trying," he said.

Over and over he repeated the words and then let out a frustrated sigh, for as usual nothing happened. Finally, he became so cross that he slammed the book shut and dust flew everywhere.

"May an old toad eat your mouldy pages!" he blurted out.

He felt thoroughly fed up and shrugged his shoulders as he turned to Alex, "Well, you can't say I didn't try. Looks like we'll have to wait until midnight after all."

He was just about to head on upstairs to take off his cloak when a familiar scratching noise could be heard. Ordompom looked up at Reema's hidey-hole, but he was nowhere to be seen.

"Meow, that's funny, I'm sure he was there a moment ago," said Pusspom.

"Oh Ordompom! You've made Reema disappear instead of me!" exclaimed Alex.

"Why bless my magic after all," he said with surprise.

Alex looked around the room, "Reema, where are you?"

Reema had come down and was sitting on the window ledge by the kitchen sink. He plucked a flora-dora flower out of the vase and waved it at them.

"Here I am," he called out and, because he was invisible, the flower appeared to be dancing in mid-air all on its own.

"Are you alright?" enquired the Wizard.

"Yes, but this is very strange," piped Reema.

"Well you know what you have to do now, don't you?" said Ordompom.

"Find the Magic Orb, of course!" replied Reema, in earnest.

"Good luck," said Alex, who was relieved that it wasn't him going over to the Yellowood Woods.

"I hope you find what you're looking for," meowed Pusspom.

"Now off you go. Take great care and return to us as soon as you can," said Ordompom, earnestly.

"I'll try my best," came the invisible reply.

Alex opened the door to the sound of Reema scampering across the floor and out into the watery sunlight.

Chapter 11.
Reema's Discovery

With Reema gone, there was nothing more to do but wait for his return. To help pass the time, Ordompom, Alex and Pusspom started to clear up the debris in the garden by removing all the dead flowers and straightening the fence. They turned over the soil to make it ready for some fresh new plants. Very hard work it was too, but they kept on going. Eventually, when the job was done, they headed back up the garden path, leaving their muddy boots on the doorstep. Once in the kitchen, they sank into comfy chairs with a big sigh of relief.

"I need a good soak in a hot bath after all that back-breaking work," groaned Ordompom.

"I've got rose thorns stuck in my fingers and they're very ouchy!" complained Alex.

"I'm covered in lumps of dried mud!" wailed Pusspom.

Ordompom went upstairs first to fill the bathtub. Lovely hot water came pouring out of the taps and Ordompom had a really good steaming soak. Then it was Alex's turn. He took off his dirty clothes and splashed about in a bath overflowing with blue bubbles. He was given a large bar of hedge blossom soap to wash with, which smelt just like flowers in the countryside. Then, to dry off, he wrapped himself in a big white fluffy towel. He felt much better after that and, as he was dressing once again, Ordompom's voice drifted up the stairs.

"I've made a fresh pot of creamy sweet corn soup and it's heating up on the stove. Would you like some Alex?"

"Oh yes please!" he called out.

Moments later they were sitting around the kitchen table tucking into the piping hot soup and some freshly baked cheese and chive bread.

Time passed as they sat there eating and chatting but there was no sign of the squirrel. Ordompom sounded concerned as he said, "Reema should have been back by now. I do hope he's alright."

Alex nodded in agreement. Not a peep had been heard from Reema all day. They continued to drink their soup. Pusspom, who was enjoying some sardines under the table, looked up when she heard a soft tapping at the back door. Alex popped out to take a look. It was dark and he couldn't see a thing. Then, he heard a familiar scratching noise on the ground.

"Is that you Reema?" He asked and felt something cool whoosh past him.

"It is, it is me!" piped an excited voice in the air.

"Oh splendid, you've returned, I'm so happy to hear your voice! You must tell us everything that happened to you!" exclaimed Ordompom.

Reema was still invisible, so he took a small red apple out of the fruit bowl and held it tightly. Now everyone could see exactly where he was and they gathered around to hear what he had to say.

"Well, it took me so long to travel to the north side of the island. I had to climb over all the fallen trees and avoid so many deep puddles. But I found the way and kept going as best I could. Finally, I arrived and went deep into the Yellowood Woods. I followed the smell of a smoky bonfire and found the camp. It was quite easy to see which was the hut of The Grizzly Grumpot, as there were two guards standing outside."

"Then what happened?' asked Alex.

"I ran up into a tree nearby and waited for someone to go inside the hut. After a while, one of those miserable Grim-Groms went through the front door and I quickly scampered in behind him. Then I sat in the corner of that damp, dark room whilst The Grizzly Grumpot and his cronies sat around an old wooden table. They argued for ages over their hateful plans for Blue Sky Island. It was hard for me to stay still for so long but, all of a sudden, the whole lot of them got up and walked out of the hut."

"Whatever happened next?" asked Alex.

"Well, while they were busy quibbling with each other, I had a good look around and noticed a rusty old cage hanging from a piece of frayed rope in the middle of the room. Once they were all gone, I scampered up the rope and guess what I found lying inside the bottom of the cage?"

"You don't mean...!" exclaimed Alex, wide-eyed.

"Yes, I do!" piped Reema.

"Are you telling me that the Magic Orb was just sitting there for all to see?" asked Ordompom.

"That's exactly what I'm saying," piped Reema.

"Jumping jellybeans, how exciting!" exclaimed Alex.

"But what on earth must The Grizzly Grumpot be thinking?" pondered Ordompom.

"Meow, what do you mean?" asked Pusspom.

"Fancy leaving it somewhere for all to see. He must have believed there were no plans to rescue the Magic Orb, otherwise he would have hidden it well out of sight."

Just as Ordompom was speaking, Reema started to become visible again but, unfortunately, only his bushy tail re-appeared. As you can imagine, he was quite annoyed about that.

"This won't do Ordompom. Where's the rest of me!" he grumbled.

"Be patient dear friend, it's um, only a matter of time." The Wizard sounded unsure but actually, Ordompom didn't have a clue how long it would take for all of Reema to come back again.

"We'll just have to make up a tale about 'The Tail Without the Squirrel!'" chuckled Alex, "Oops sorry Reema, only joking!"

The squirrel squealed at him indignantly.

"Anyway, well done Reema for finding the Magic Orb. We really should go back to the Yellowood Woods, but sadly that's not going to be tonight. I'm pooped after all that hard work in the garden and I just can't conjure up any magic right now. What we need is a good night's rest to prepare us for the big challenge tomorrow," said Ordompom.

A little later, after Alex had gone to bed, Ordompom was relaxing in his chair by the fire. He rocked back and forth with Pusspom curled up on his lap. He stroked her fur and watched the logs burning in the grate. Speaking softly, he said,

"Pusspom, there is something important I have to discuss with all of you in the morning before we go to the Grizzly Grumpot's camp and I'll explain everything tomorrow."

"I'm a bit too sleepy to hear anything more now anyway," she purred.

"It's about time for me to go to bed as well," said the Wizard, as he took off his glasses and rubbed his tired eyes. It was very tempting to fall asleep in front of the glowing embers but slowly he eased himself out of his rocking chair and gently put Pusspom into her basket.

"Goodnight Pusspom," he said, stroking her one more time before shutting the kitchen door and heading for bed.

Chapter 12.

Making Plans For
What's To Come

Very early the next morning there was a lot of noise outside Alex's bedroom door. He woke up with a start and leapt out of bed, running into the corridor to see what the commotion was all about. There, he found Pusspom hissing, with her back arched and her fur standing on end. Reema (who was now fully visible again), was bobbing around like a frantic hamster on a wheel. They were both acting so strangely that Alex had to find out why.

"What on earth's the matter with you two?" he demanded.

"Something peculiar is falling out of the sky. Come quickly and see!" screeched Reema.

Alex returned to his bedroom and flung back the curtains. He pressed his nose against the windowpane and blurted out, "Gee whizz! It's snowing. How wonderful - I *love* snow!"

"Snow? What's snow? I've never seen snow before," wailed Pusspom.

"Well, when it gets cold enough, rain turns into frozen white flakes and that's just what you can see. Look how fast the snow is falling! Now that's what I call a flurry in a hurry!!" exclaimed Alex with delight.

"Meow, what ghastly stuff. Make it go away! It has never been cold enough to snow on Blue Sky Island before, but now everything is covered in a frosty white blanket. Pour a bucket of hot water all over it to make it melt! I want my warm sunshine back," said Pusspom.

They heard the kitchen door open and went downstairs to find Ordompom tapping the snow off his boots. He had just come in from shovelling the cold white powdery stuff away from the garden path.

"B-r-r-r-r, it's freezing cold and extremely icy out there! The Grizzly Grumpot is up to his tricks again. When will this folly ever end?!" he growled through chattering teeth, as he brushed the snow off his bobble hat. Alex tried to comfort him by offering some breakfast.

"How would you like some hot porridge with golden syrup?" he asked.

"Oooh yes please. And a nice mug of tea too, that would be just the ticket!" replied Ordompom gratefully.

Ordompom stood in front of the warm stove to thaw himself out whilst Alex got busy. It wasn't long before the Wizard was wrapping his frozen fingers around a large mug of piping hot tea and tucking into a delicious bowl of syrupy porridge.

"My friends, we have to talk about plans for this evening. First of all, I'm going to try really hard to make *you* invisible Alex." He paused for a bit and then he spoke slowly, "There is something else too."

"Whatever is that?" asked Alex.

"We have to create a distraction."

"I don't understand."

"Well, once you are invisible and have returned to the Yellowood Woods, you should be able to get into

The Grizzly Grumpot's hut fairly easily. But to recover the Magic Orb without The Grizzly Grumpot realising something's up ... well that's another matter. So, we have to find a way to keep the coast clear by creating some kind of diversion. Then Alex, you can take the Magic Orb and escape without any trouble. Now then, if any of you three have any ideas about what to do, it would be most helpful," said Ordompom, looking at them seriously.

It went quiet as they all sat around the table thinking hard.

Suddenly Alex blurted out, "I've got it!" It made everybody jump and they leant forward to hear what he had to say.

"I have a plan that might just work." He whispered his idea to them. At first, they didn't quite understand what he was talking about but, as he explained some more, they started to smile. By the time he'd finished telling them what his idea was, they were all falling about with laughter.

"So, what do you think?" beamed Alex.

"Yes, oh yes – I like it! That's settled then. We'll use your plan tonight and see what happens," roared Ordompom with glee.

The decision had been made and they all left the kitchen table. By now it had stopped snowing and Alex decided to go outside and throw some snowballs. Pusspom was not amused when one or two of the snowballs whizzed past and narrowly missed her. She stayed well out of the way after that. Reema sat on the fence as usual and watched Alex enjoying himself, but he soon scampered back inside as it was far too cold for him. Gradually, the sun came out and the snow quickly melted away. It turned into a warm and pleasant afternoon, just like all the other days on Blue Sky Island. Alex had had his fun and now the snow was all but gone.

As dusk was falling, Ordompom wanted to cast his spell and get Alex over to the Grizzly Grumpot's camp as soon as possible. The Wizard was impatient to start the proceedings so he gathered everyone up and they stepped into the garden. As Pusspom and Reema watched on curiously, Alex stood in front of Ordompom and he waved his mystical magic wand around.

"IN THE BRIGHTNESS OF THE DAY,
OR THE DARKNESS OF THE NIGHT,
TO MAKE SOMEBODY DISAPPEAR,
I CAST THIS SPELL WITH ALL MY MIGHT."

"IN THE BRIGHTNESS OF THE DAY,
OR THE DARKNESS OF THE NIGHT..."

Ordompom's voice floated through the air. He repeated the spell three times with his eyes shut and continued to wave his magic wand with enthusiasm. When he opened his eyes again, he was rather surprised – but very relieved – to see that Alex had actually disappeared.

"Blizzards and Wizards! My spell has worked the very first time!" said Ordompom. He was feeling so pleased with himself.

"Meow and hello, Alex, where are you?" called out Pusspom.

"I'm over here by the Hairy Fairy Moss," came Alex's voice, "And this is most strange. Why, I can't even see my hands in front of my face..."

"Now you know just what it feels like!" piped Reema indignantly.

Ordompom dug deep into the pocket of his robe and pulled out a small silvery box.

"Alex, I want you to carry this with you." He held out the shiny box.

"What's this for?" asked Alex.

"I'll explain," said Ordompom. "Take a close look and you will see a button on the side of the box. Press the button and it will light up like a torch. Lead the way to the Grizzly Grumpot's camp and we'll follow you Alex. When you're near to the Yellowood Woods be sure to switch off the beam of light. We will still just be able to see the silvery box reflected in the moonlight. We'll find somewhere to hide in the woods as we put your little diversion plan into action. Whilst that's happening, slip into the Grizzly Grumpot's hut and take the Magic Orb as quickly as you can. When we see the silvery box re-appear, that will mean you have the Magic Orb and then we can head on back to the cottage!"

"Sounds like a jolly good plan to me," said Pusspom.

Alex came forward and took the box from Ordompom, which was quite a funny sight to behold because it really did look like the box was hovering in the air, all on its own.

"Now then everyone, are we ready to go?" asked Ordompom.

"Well I certainly am," said invisible Alex, in a loud, clear voice.

"Me too," said Pusspom, and flicked her tail.

"I'm ready as well!" piped Reema, as he scampered along the fence.

Chapter 13.

A Surprise For
The Grim-Groms!

The night had become dark, except for a bright banana-shaped moon in the sky. Alex held the silvery box out in front of him. It shone a ray of light in the darkness as he led Ordompom, Pusspom and Reema towards the Grizzly Grumpot's camp. When they arrived at the edge of the Yellowood Woods, Alex remembered to switch off his beam of light. Then they carefully weaved their way through the forbidding trees in search of a bush to hide behind. Most of the bushes had dried brown leaves on them but, luckily, they found the only big thick bush left in the woods and they crouched down behind it in the shadows.

Ordompom pushed the leaves apart to see what was going on. He spied a handful of Grim-Groms sitting around a smoky campfire. They were singing their favourite miserable songs so badly it sounded just like cats wailing. Pusspom wanted to join in too, but knew she couldn't as she had to keep quiet. In another corner of the camp, a couple of Grim-Groms were chopping up dead trees for firewood. Two more were picking up the roughly cut pieces of wood and dropping them onto an untidy pile, in readiness for the next bonfire.

It wasn't long before a very round Grim-Grom came waddling along with a heavy tray full of food and they watched as he headed towards the huts nearby. The puffing green creature stopped outside the biggest hut of all, where Grim-Groms Joscal and Tilano were standing on guard.

"That's the Grizzly Grumpot's hut," whispered Reema.

The very round Grim-Grom spoke a few words to the guards before he went inside, staggering under the weight of the heavy tray. The door closed behind him and, moments later, he came out again, having emptied the tray of its contents.

"I wonder what The Grizzly Grumpot eats," said Alex quietly.

"I can tell you what he had on his plate the day I was in his hut. Roasted slug sausages on a bed of slimy seaweed, with stale kale stalks and some beetle fritters dipped in brown mud ketchup. And when he'd eaten all that, he washed down some creepy cupcakes with a large glass of bitter bonberry juice!" piped Reema.

"Ugh, that sounds perfectly disgusting!" exclaimed Alex.

"Shhh, keep your voice down," whispered Ordompom. "Now then, it's time to put our little diversion plan into action. Alex, I want you to think very hard about the special surprise we have for our friends over there and I will try to 'magic it up'."

Ordompom waved his mystical magic wand in the air and waited for something to happen. Quite soon, he heard a new sound in the distance. He listened harder. Sure enough there it was, *exactly* the sound he was hoping for, all merry and musical, and it filled the evening air.

Suddenly the Grim-Groms, who were sitting around the smoky campfire, stopped their awful singing and jumped up in fright. For coming towards them was something they had never seen before and it looked like a great big, musical box on wheels. Two powerful beams of light shone out from the front of the brightly coloured box. The cheerful tinkling music continued as the dazzling lights came closer. The Grim-Groms linked arms to form a wall against this strange enemy.

They were very scared, but Alex and his friends knew better and were happy to see such a sight. For guess what? Ordompom had managed to 'magic up' an ice-cream van!

As the ice-cream van ground to a halt, so too did the music. Sitting behind the steering wheel of the van was a jolly looking man wearing a green shirt covered with big white polka dots and a flat cap to match. He was smiling from ear to ear as he leant out of the driver's window and said in a cheerful manner,

"A very good evening to you all. My name is Mr Fred. I'm the ice-cream man and this here is my ice-cream van. Now then, who would like a Chunky-Chocolate-Chuckle-On-A-Stick?" He paused for a second and then continued, "Or maybe you fancy a Cracking Caramelicious Cone?"

There was total silence as the Grim-Groms stared at him in disbelief and blinked their bright orange eyes. Mr Fred repeated his question more slowly and still he beamed at them.

One of the braver Grim-Groms stepped forward and called out, "What's a Choco Chucklie or a Crackling Caramule?"

Mr Fred laughed out loud.

"Why, they're ice-creams and lollies of course! Don't tell me you've never had an ice-cream before. Come on over here right now and try one of my chilly delights. They're absolutely delicious!!"

With that, he got out the driver's seat and slid open the side window for business. Pointing to a brave Grim-Grom and beckoning him over, he said,

"You Sir, step right up and have something out of my ice-box. How's about a Mumbo Jumbo Mango Muncher. Just think Sir, ripe mango sauce swirled together with dairy vanilla ice-cream and fruity mango pieces. What could be more heavenly?" He raised his eyes to the sky and gave a lengthy sigh.

The Grim-Grom was uneasy, but curiosity got the better of him. He and the others started gathering slowly around the van. Bossy Joscal pushed them out of the way to get to the front of the queue. He wanted to be the first to try one of these mysterious new sweet treats.

"Be ready to protect me in case it's a trap," he whispered to Tilano. Then he looked at the colourful pictures of ice-creams and fruit-flavoured lollies stuck on the van's window.

"I'll try one of those," he said glumly, pointing to a Luscious Lemon Lolly. Mr Fred dug deep into his freezer. He took out the lolly and handed it to Joscal.

"There's no charge tonight, Sir. All the ice-creams and lollies are on me. Absolutely free!" he grinned at Joscal.

Joscal turned 'the thing' over in his hand.

"It's cold," he wailed.

"Of course it's cold. Now then, you bite into that and tell me what you think. And, if you don't say it's absolutely yummy, I'll eat my hat!"

He watched as the Grim-Grom tried to put the lolly into his mouth.

"No, no, Sir not like that! You have to take the wrapper off first."

Joscal removed the crinkly silver paper and slowly sank his teeth into the scrumptious treat. Mr Fred watched, expecting him to be delighted, but instead, to Mr Fred's dismay, Joscal burst into tears.

"Oh deary, deary me, what on earth's wrong?" said Mr Fred.

"This icy lump *is* very tasty just like you said. That's why I'm so happy," snivelled the mournful Grim-Grom, wiping a tear away from his eye.

"What a strange creature," thought Mr Fred, looking puzzled. He didn't know about Grim-Groms being sad when they're happy.

At that very moment The Grizzly Grumpot flung open his hut door and stormed out.

"What *is* going on here? Who dares to come to my side of Bloo Sky Island and not be afraid!" he snarled in his nastiest voice.

A chirpy voice filled the air and The Grizzly Grumpot could not believe his ears.

"You, Sir, come on over here, Sir. Don't be shouting now. You must try one of my ice-creams! You'll not be disappointed because they are the best!"

Then Mr Fred announced proudly, "I've won awards and prizes for all my extra special flavours. Come along now, don't be shy."

The Grizzly Grumpot was FURIOUS at being disturbed. He stomped over to Mr Fred's van to send him packing!

Ordompom and the others watched the amusing scene happening before them. This was exactly the moment they had been waiting for.

"Right then Alex, it's time for you to go and recover the Magic Orb. Go, go now and the best of luck to you," whispered Ordompom.

Invisible Alex stood up straight and tall (not that anyone could see him), and swiftly made his way over to the Grizzly Grumpot's hut.

There were no guards outside and the place was completely deserted thanks to Mr Fred. Alex tiptoed into the hut and looked around cautiously as he was more than a little bit afraid. It was dark and damp and there were cobwebs everywhere. The place smelt of something quite horrible and he soon realised what it was. A plate of half-eaten slug sausages and slimy seaweed was lying on the floor. It was revolting. Alex really didn't like that smell and so he held his nose. Next to the disgusting plate of food lay the Grizzly Grumpot's makeshift bed of sparrow feathers. In one corner of the room he noticed the dripping candle on an upturned crate, which cast ghostly shadows on the wall. In the middle of the room he saw a rusty old cage hanging down on a fraying piece of rope, just the way Reema had described it. As he approached, he saw a soft glowing light inside the cage. He took a closer look and there, nestling in some straw, sat the precious Magic Orb.

"Cripes and Capers!" said Alex out loud as he spotted the Orb, "I can't believe it. The Magic Orb is still here."

He wasted no time and found a rickety three-legged stool to stand on. Steadying himself, he reached up to untie the rope. As he wrapped his arms around the cage, he felt a wonderful magical power radiating from it. But, oh my goodness, just as he was about to step down, the stool collapsed beneath him with a resounding crash! Alex fell to the floor and lay there, still clutching the cage. He groaned and saw stars swirling around his head. Gradually he sat up and looked inside the cage and was relieved to see the Magic Orb had not been damaged. Then he listened earnestly just in case anyone had heard him fall. But all he could hear in the distance was some muffled shouting going on between Mr Fred and The Grizzly Grumpot.

"Phew, that was close," he thought to himself.

With wobbly legs he stood up and brushed himself down (which is a bit difficult to do when you're invisible). He placed the Magic Orb in the silvery box and left the empty cage behind. He looked around the room once more, before slipping out of the hut whilst the coast was still clear.

"Gadzooks! No more Grottynots here," he said to himself.

He crept away and was silently making his way back to the others, when he thought he could hear some low moaning noises coming from somewhere close by and within the trees. Alex cautiously followed the sound through the bare branches. There, he stumbled across a large old hut with filthy windows and iron bars fixed in front of them. He could barely see through the dirty panes of glass. But what Alex saw next shocked him. Some sad-looking people were sitting on the floor in a dimly lit room. They were obviously being held prisoner, because the poor folk were behind a heavy metal door with an enormous padlock.

"Rockets and Revelations! These must be the islanders who disappeared!" exclaimed Alex, under his breath. Then he said with determination, "I'm not leaving without them!"

He looked to the left and then to the right. There were no Grim-Groms lurking around, so he walked straight up to the huge door and tapped on it.

"Who's there?" whispered a shaky voice from within.

"My name is Alex. I'm a friend of Ordompom's and I'm going to help you escape from this place," he said, urgently.

The bewildered islanders looked at one another. There were about ten of them in that dirty room and they were thoroughly fed up with being held captive.

"You have to help me. Do you know where the key is to unlock the door?" asked Alex.

Peering through a slit in the door one of the villagers said, "Look behind you. Over there are a bunch of keys hanging on the tree."

Alex turned around and saw the keys hanging on a large branch. He reached up, took them down and, while the islanders waited patiently, he tried one key at a time. "Oh rats!" he exclaimed, with each key that wouldn't open the door. Wouldn't you know it, the very last key was the one that turned in the lock. It was bothersome and stiff but eventually it did turn and, with an enormous effort, he pulled at the heavy door. The islanders blinked as the door opened slowly as if by magic, because no one was standing on the other side of it. All they could see was a bright silvery box seemingly floating in the air.

"Sorry folks, I've had an invisible spell cast over me by Ordompom. But don't worry, I will re-appear later." Then Alex added hastily, "The guards will be back soon, so we must leave at once. There is no time to lose – hurry! hurry!"

One by one the dishevelled islanders struggled to their feet and shuffled out of the hut. They followed Alex as he carried the precious box, which lit the way before them.

"No more Grottynots here!" he said to himself once again.

Meanwhile back at the ice-cream van, Ordompom, Pusspom and Reema continued hiding behind the bush whilst waiting for Alex to return. Pusspom could see very clearly with her cat's eyes in the dark and so was the first to see Alex's torchlight re-appear in the distance, with a line of people trailing behind it. Pusspom pointed with her paw.

"Look, look over there. Where did all those people come from Ordompom?"

"They are the missing islanders! Alex must have rescued them. This is great news!" he whispered.

"I hope the Magic Orb has been rescued too," piped Reema.

"I think it has. Can you see that glow coming from Alex's box? It *must* be the Magic Orb," said the Wizard, with relief.

"Hurrah and whoopee!" blurted out Reema too loudly, as he bobbed up and down with excitement.

"Shhh Reema. I know you're excited, but now we have what we came for, it's time to get out of here," urged Ordompom.

And so it was, that Alex and the small group of islanders quietly slipped away from the campsite with Ordompom, Pusspom and Reema close behind. Disappearing under the blanket of darkness, they glanced back once at the extraordinary scene by the ice-cream van. They were just in time to see Mr Fred tipping a bowl of warm chocolate sauce over the Grizzly Grumpot's head. He was shouting at him,

"If you don't like my wonderful icy treats you rude Grumpy Grizzleplop then here's some sauce for you! Harrumph!"

And, with that, Mr Fred and his merry tinkling van vanished into thin air!

The Grizzly Grumpot could not quite believe what had just happened to him and he was livid! No matter how hard he tried, he could not get the sweet, sticky stuff off his head. By the time he returned to his hut and found the empty cage on the floor with the Magic Orb gone, it was too late to do anything about it. He was even more furious when he discovered the islanders had been rescued too. So instead he had to make do with yelling at the Grim-Groms.

"Call yourselves guards? You're more like a bunch of bumble-heads! I've never known such a useless cluster of quiverin' clots!! You were supposed to guard that Orby thing and now it's gone, gone, gone!"

The Grim-Groms stood there quaking as The Grizzly Grumpot ranted on. "And what has happened to all those island folk you were supposed to be guardin' too? Gone, gone, gone!" He shook both his hairy fists at them. Then he stormed into his hut and slammed the door so hard that some dried mud fell through the roof onto the floor below, narrowly missing him. He could be heard stomping around his room in a rage, yelling diddly-squat at the top of his voice.

Chapter 14.

Time To Fly

The next morning found the sun shining down on Blue Sky Island. In his cottage, Ordompom noticed his toes sticking out at the end of the bedcover and he wiggled them with happiness. Last night's adventure made him hum, "Yahoo-be-doo, be-doo-yahoo, we've got the Magic Orb!"

He didn't linger long and slipped out bed, still humming as he went. Another busy day lay ahead.

"Come on Alex, time to get up," he called out.

Alex leapt out of bed and went straight to the mirror. He was very relieved to see his reflection staring back at him. Ordompom's spell had worn off and he was 'all there' once again. He dressed and when he came out of his bedroom, was surprised to see Ordompom in his wizard's clothes.

"My, how grand you look," said Alex, as he admired Ordompom's finest silky cloak.

"This is 'Rescue Orion' Day, so I'm celebrating by wearing my best gear," he said, proudly. In one pocket of his cloak he'd tucked the Magic Orb and in the other was his mystical magic wand. Then he carefully placed the glossy black wizard's hat on his head.

Downstairs by the backdoor, Pusspom and Reema were ready and waiting to go.

"Meow, this *is* a very special day," purred Pusspom.

"Yes, it is exciting, it is very exciting," piped Reema.

Alex came into the kitchen and he was smiling.

"Did you see how much the Grim-Groms enjoyed their ice lollies last night!" he chuckled.

"We did indeed. But enough of that now, it's time to hurry along to the Many-a-Moon Clock Tower. I'm sure Orion will be very pleased to see us," said Ordompom with enthusiasm.

He beckoned everyone to leave the house and they walked briskly along Linden Lane towards the village. It was still early and nobody else was up yet. Even the village square was completely deserted. In a short while they stopped in front of the Many-a-Moon Clock Tower and looked up as far as the eye could see. Poor Orion was still stuck right at the top on his solitary perch.

"Ordompom?" said Alex, "I have a question for you."

"Yes Alex, what is it?"

"How are we going to get the Magic Orb all the way up to Orion?" he asked.

Ordompom turned to Alex and looked at him seriously. Then he spoke. "I was about to ask if you would like to take it up there for me. After all you do have your magical dezora around you."

"How on earth would I get up there?" queried Alex.

"Well ... it just so happens I have a flying spell on me and I'm feeling so good this morning, I'm sure it will work," said Ordompom, enthusiastically.

"Pigs might fly, but not me, not on my own! Really Ordompom, how could you think such a thing!"

"You flew here with Orion's Messenger, didn't you?"

"Yes, but that was different. I was holding on to a splendid falcon and I couldn't possibly have made that journey without him," he gasped.

"Well, why shouldn't you fly? You never know, you might enjoy it," coaxed Ordompom.

"I'm really not keen on this idea of yours Ordompom," said Alex, his voice filled with uncertainty.

"Alex, it was you who rescued the Magic Orb, so it is only right and proper that *you* should be the one to rescue Orion too. And anyway, I think it would be a good idea for someone young and energetic to fly up to the top of the Clock Tower," said the Wizard.

"What if the spell doesn't work properly?" asked Alex.

"Well … if you found yourself suddenly falling down to earth again…" Ordompom stopped mid-sentence and looked around, "I'd say aim for the duck pond over there." He pointed eagerly towards the pond in the middle of the village green.

Alex didn't wait a second before replying, "Tumbling terrapins! This is one time when I really can't help you Ordompom. I'm covered in bruises from that fall in the Grizzly Grumpot's hut yesterday and now you're telling me that I might end up in the duck pond too! No thank you!" he exclaimed.

"Oh dear, I was hoping you would agree," sighed Ordompom.

"I have a better idea. How about sending Pusspom up instead? After all, cats are supposed to have nine lives," suggested Alex.

The black and white cat had been sitting there listening to them and she suddenly became alarmed.

"Meow, no not me! I don't mind heights, but I hate water and would not like to end up in the duck pond either!" she hissed.

"Come on Pusspom, a clever cat like you could manage to land safely, I'm sure of that," said Alex stroking her between the ears.

"Me-e-e-o-o-w," wailed Pusspom, waving her tail sharply, "What about Reema going up the Clock Tower instead of me?" Reema looked shocked.

"No, no, I'm not a flying squirrel!" he squealed with dismay, "And I'm far too small to carry the Magic Orb all that way!"

All eyes were fixed on Pusspom again. "Oh, come on, Pusspom, please do it for us, p -l -e -a -s -e," implored Ordompom.

Pusspom continued to wave her tail sharply.

"Oh, I suppose so, but I'm not happy about it," she meowed.

"Right then, that's settled," said Ordompom, briskly.

He gave the Magic Orb to Pusspom, and she put it between her paws. Ordompom stood there, waved his mystical magic wand and began to chant the magic spell:

"I'M POINTING UPWARD TO THE SKY,
IN THAT DIRECTION YOU MUST FLY.
AS IF WITH WINGS YOU'LL MAKE NO SOUND,
WHEN YOU TAKE OFF AND LEAVE THE GROUND.
LIKE A BIRD BE SWIFT AND FREE,
TO FIND THE PLACE YOU NEED TO BE.
AND IN THE AIR WHEN YOU ARE HIGH,
DON'T STOP TO WAVE AS YOU FLY BY."

As always, he repeated the spell three times and everyone held their breath as Pusspom stood perfectly still and rooted to the spot.

'Your spell has to work today Ordompom, you must make Pusspom fly!' Alex's eyes were shut tight and he wished very hard.

Ordompom continued to repeat the spell but, finally, he stopped waving his wand around. The usual thing had happened – yes, you've guessed it, absolutely nothing!

"Oh dear, whatever am I to do?" he sighed and shrugged his shoulders.

Well there wasn't much he could do was there? Except perhaps to go back to the cottage and consult with the Galactic Rocks again. Ordompom was about to make that suggestion when Alex spoke to him.

"You know, the best time to cast your spell is in the middle of the night, so if your magic isn't working now, then you'll have to try again later," he encouraged.

"I'm really worried, Alex. If we don't get the Magic Orb up to Orion very soon, the Grizzly Grumpot will be heading this way and hammering at our front door!" said Ordompom, looking at him very seriously.

"What makes you think that?" asked Alex.

"Well, we snatched the Magic Orb from under his nose and rescued the islanders too. If that wasn't bad enough, all those goings-on with the ice-cream man last night will have made him as hopping mad as a kangaroo!"

"Oh that's true!" said Alex.

"The one thing that will ensure The Grizzly Grumpot can stay on Blue Sky Island is the Magic Orb. He'll be coming over to get it before you can say, 'Sham-abam-adrat, don't do that!"

Ordompom wrung his hands together and was really upset that the flying spell hadn't worked. He turned to his friends and said forlornly, "I'm so sorry. I did try my best."

Ordompom was about to head for home but, as he spoke, he was completely unaware that his cloak had started to move all on its own. It was rippling ever so gently, as if it were being blown in a breeze.

"What's happening to your cloak? Look, look it's doing peculiar things!" exclaimed Alex.

Ordompom was mystified as to why his cloak was moving and now it was flapping about.

"Oh my, oh my, whatever is going on?" Suddenly he realised what was happening and he shouted to Pusspom.

"Be quick, give me the Magic Orb. I feel like I'm about to take off! Pusspom be q-u-i-c-k!!"

Pusspom darted over with the Magic Orb and Ordompom looked down to find his feet walking on air.

"I can't stay on the ground any longer! This is not what I expected. Me? Flying? At my time of life? Oh my, oh my!" he exclaimed.

It was quite a sight to see as Ordompom rose up into the sky. His cloak was now floating gracefully all around him. Higher and higher he went, above the houses, right to the top of the Many-a-Moon Clock Tower.

"My goodness me, I'm going to miss Orion altogether if I carry on travelling at this speed!"

And he nearly did too! But just as his legs were floating on up past him, he managed to grab onto Orion's perch. Without a moment to lose, he took his belt and tied himself to Mr Many-a-Moon. Then he fumbled around inside his pocket and took out the Magic Orb. He held it up in his hand and the magical ball glittered brightly in the sunlight.

"You have been waiting such a long time for this moment," Ordompom whispered to Orion.

With great care, he placed the Magic Orb between Orion's talons and, as he did so, a small teardrop appeared in the corner of the eagle's ruby red eye.

"There, there, it's time to set you free now," said Ordompom.

He expected Orion to move, but the great bird remained completely still. Ordompom held on to Mr Many-a-Moon and didn't know quite what to do next.

"Well, I can't just float around here waiting for something to happen, so I'd better get back to the others," he said out loud. He could see Alex, Pusspom and Reema like tiny specks on the ground and suddenly realised just how high up he was. He gave Orion one last wistful look and watched him carefully to see if there were any signs of movement. Orion was fixed to the spot and so Ordompom undid the belt which had secured him to Mr Many-a-Moon. Ever so slowly he let go and, to his immense relief, he started floating downwards.

"Now I know what it feels like to be a leaf falling in the autumn," he thought to himself, as he gently swayed from side to side. The pleasant feeling didn't last for too long though, because he started to pick up speed. Faster and faster he whizzed, with the air whistling around his ears. Just in time, he remembered to look for the duck pond and, as he continued to plummet down, he exclaimed,

"Where is it, where is that duck pond. A-a-r-r-argh!!"

There was an almighty SPLASH! He landed right in the middle of the pond! Crystal droplets shot up into the air like a dancing fountain and water lilies exploded in all directions. The pond wasn't deep and fortunately there were not many ducks paddling around at the time. Ordompom just sat there spluttering. His hat had managed to stay on, but it was oh-so crumpled and sat on his head at a most peculiar angle. Alex, Pusspom and Reema came rushing over to help pull Ordompom out. He was soaked and looked thoroughly bedraggled as he tried to straighten his hat.

"Are you alright?" asked Alex anxiously.

"I-I-I'm not sure," spluttered Ordompom, as he spat out a mouthful of pond water and a tadpole. Struggling to his feet, he steadied himself and, with Alex's help, he climbed out of the pond. Then he sat down on a wooden bench nearby and squeezed some water out of his sopping cloak. Pusspom meowed and Reema bobbed around, both of them fussing over the Wizard as he tried to get his breath back.

"Thank you for your assistance dear friends, I'm very relieved to be back in one piece. But I do need to get out of these dreadfully wet clothes."

Ordompom looked towards the clock tower hoping to see some movement from Orion. Sadly, it was not to be.

"Let's go back to the cottage then," he sighed.

Chapter 15.

The News Is Not Good

As Alex, Pusspom and Reema helped Ordompom move slowly away from the duck pond, they noticed a small group of people walking towards them. Alex immediately realised who they were.

"Oh Ordompom, here come the islanders, the ones we rescued from the Grizzly Grumpot's camp last night!" he declared.

"I wonder what they want," said Ordompom, still feeling shaky after his soggy mishap. Drip, drip, drop, the water fell off his hat as he tried to put on a brave face. A young man from the group came striding over. He was not too tall, with a mop of golden-brown hair and freckles on his face.

"Hello, I'm Doren and on behalf of the islanders here," he swept his hand around, "We are so grateful for being rescued. It was very daring of this boy to come and get us," he said, pointing to Alex. "You could have walked away but instead you took an enormous risk to help us. We think you are a hero and want to say a great big thank you."

With that, Doren grabbed Alex's hand and pumped it up and down vigorously.

Ordompom smiled, "My friend, you are right. What Alex did was most commendable and he certainly banished the Grottynots by rescuing you all. He has also been most helpful in our mission to get rid of The Grizzly Grumpot."

"Well ... Ordompom, that's another reason why I'm here. There is big trouble brewing!" blurted out Doren.

"Whatever do you mean?" asked Ordompom.

"Earlier this morning, when I looked out of my window, I noticed The Grizzly Grumpot and his gang of Grim-Groms marching through the Rolling Green Hills.

They were heading in our direction *and* carrying some rather nasty looking swords! I rushed out of the house to warn the islanders. That's when I spotted you, Ordompom, floating up in the air." Doren beckoned towards the islanders, "So all together, we came here to warn you."

"This is disastrous!" exclaimed Alex.

"Something like this was bound to happen. The Magic Orb has not had its magical power renewed and even though I gave it back to Orion, he is still stuck on top of the Many-a-Moon Clock Tower," said Ordompom, gravely, as Alex, Pusspom and Reema nodded in agreement.

"What can we do now? None of us have any weapons and we're no match for The Grizzly Grumpot!" said Doren.

Ordompom thought for a moment and then he spoke urgently.

"I have an idea. There is a large gardening shed under the old oak tree on the village green. Run over there Doren and take some helpers with you. Raid the shed for tools and bring them back here. We'll arm ourselves with spades and pitch forks, brooms and shovels. They may not be much use against swords, but they'll be better than nothing!"

"Let's do it immediately!" said Doren in earnest.

He called the others to follow him and started running off in the direction of the shed to see what he could find. By now, more people were gathering around the duck pond, including Miss Candy Pink. She waved at Alex, but today she was not smiling as she said to him, "Now you know the reason why you were called to the island Alex. You have to help us as beat this dark and evil monster."

The place was very crowded by the time Doren and the others came back, pushing wheelbarrows piled high with gardening tools.

Still dripping, Ordompom stood on the bench so that everyone could see him and he clapped his hands together. The islanders stopped talking and listened to what Ordompom had to say.

"Good people of Blue Sky Island. Great danger is coming our way. We are about to face the worst threat to our peace and happiness. Please take these tools to defend yourselves and be prepared to fight. We must stand together to safeguard our precious island!"

There was an immediate frenzy as tools were grabbed and passed around. Ordompom stepped down from the bench, with rivulets of water still falling from his sloshy cloak. As he did so, he thought he heard a strange sound. He gazed up at Orion, to see if the beautiful bird had taken to the air, but there was no sign of movement. He listened harder. This was not a noise that he or any of the islanders had ever heard before. They all looked to where the noise was coming from right on the other side of the village green. Rockety-clump! Rockety-clump! Rockety-clump!

"Oh my, oh my," gasped Ordompom, for in the distance was a most shocking sight. It was The Grizzly Grumpot, heading towards them with great big swaggering steps so heavy that the ground shook. Behind him, with their swords held high, were hordes of Grim-Groms. Their eyes were like blazing orange balls and The Grizzly Grumpot had mustered every last one of them for this confrontation. They came forward marching in such a strange way – Rockety-clump! Rockety-clump! Rockety-clump!

Ordompom was holding a large gardening fork and he stood there trembling. Alex watched the oncoming invaders anxiously, whilst clutching a wooden spade.

Pusspom was terrified and hid beneath the Wizard's cloak and, as for Reema, he certainly didn't like what he saw and quickly scurried up into a tree nearby. Every last islander held something to whack the intruders with, as the thundering noise continued to get louder and louder.

Once they were close by, The Grizzly Grumpot raised his sword in the air and the Grim-Groms knocked into one another as they ground to an untidy halt. At the very back of this giant-sized group was a row of Grim-Groms holding large catapults. The Grizzly Grumpot yelled a command to them,

"Rear guard, aim and fire!" Before anyone knew it, a hailstorm of mud the size of tennis balls came flying over. Most of the mud balls missed their mark, but cries of pain could be heard from the few people that had been hit. The Grizzly Grumpot lumbered forward and, when he finally stopped, he was so near to Ordompom they could almost rub noses! Everything went completely quiet and Ordompom looked up at The Grizzly Grumpot from under his squishy, sopping hat.

Alex wondered what was going to happen next. He didn't have to wait long for the eerie silence to be broken.

The Grizzly Grumpot boomed out, "YOU 'orrible wizard YOU! YOU thought YOU were so clever when YOU sneaked into MY camp, invaded MY home and stole that sparklin' Orby thing from ME!!"

Ordompom opened his mouth as though he was about to say something but thought better of it and shut his mouth again.

"I'll bet you had a good laugh last night when me and the Grim-Groms were tricked into tryin' that frozen stuff-on-a-stick!" He yelled and waved his sword threateningly in the air. The Grim-Groms joined in and swung their swords about too. He continued, "I HATE that revoltin', icy, mushy muck! And, as for the infuriatin' bloke who covered me with all that sticky chocolate sauce, how DARE he! Well now it's my turn and you lot are goin' to regret it!"

The villagers were petrified as The Grizzly Grumpot glared at them and ranted on as he pointed towards the Many-a-Moon Clock Tower with his sword.

"That big bird up there and that Orby thing are completely useless to you!"

Then he yelled at Ordompom, "Your old spells are a waste of time you Worthless Wiltin' Wizard! And, as for you, Bothersome Boy...!" he snarled at Alex and poked him in the chest with a hairy finger.

"Hey, stop that!" shouted Alex, surprising himself for being so bold. At this point he would rather have been back home tucked up safely in his own bed but, instead, here he was, facing a snarling beast of an ogre and lots of menacing swords.

"Don't you DARE raise your voice to me, the one who is now lord and master of Bloo Sky Island!" growled The Grizzly Grumpot at him. He turned to the islanders, raised his huge fist in anger and shook it at them.

"That first attack of mud balls was just a warnin' to you. Go back to your homes, all of you. There's no use in fightin' because you cannot win and more of you will get hurt. You'd better get used to the idea that I'm here to stay and things are goin' to be *very* different from now on!"

The islanders looked dismayed as The Grizzly Grumpot commanded the Grim-Groms to send over

THE NEWS IS NOT GOOD

another volley of the rock-hard mud balls. There were more cries of pain as the missiles hit their mark. Then The Grizzly Grumpot yelled, "Seize the Wizard and the Boy! Take them prisoner and I shall decide what to do with them once we get back to my encampment."

Everyone watched with horror as Ordompom and Alex were surrounded by lots of sword-thrusting Grim-Groms, who made the pair stand back to back, whilst Joscal and Tilano chained them together. Pusspom tried to escape by running out from underneath Ordompom's cloak. She was immediately pounced upon by a nimble Grim-Grom, who bundled her into the very same rusty cage that had held the Magic Orb only the day before. As for Reema, he was still hiding up in the tree nearby, shaking with fear as he watched the goings-on down below.

The Grizzly Grumpot had a sly look on his face. "Do you know what? I think I'm goin' to turn the prisoners into black parakeets. Then they can squawk all they like whilst I'm eatin' my supper," he sneered.

Ordompom and Alex looked at each other with alarm and there was an angry rumbling amongst the islanders. Doren boldly stepped forward to speak.

"You leave them alone! D'you hear me?! Unchain them at once!" he yelled at The Grizzly Grumpot.

"You are too brave for one who has already been my prisoner. Don't provoke me further or you'll be chained up too!" growled The Grizzly Grumpot menacingly.

"I'm not afraid of you and nor are my friends. This is our island and we will not give it up without a fight!" shouted Doren defiantly.

The Islanders and Doren started making lots of noise by banging and clanging their gardening tools on the

109

ground and stomping their feet. As they did so they began to chant:

"GRIM-GROMS OUT – HEAR US SHOUT!
PACK YOUR BAGS AND TURNABOUT!
GRIZZLY GRUMPOT YOU GO TOO!
BLUE SKY ISLAND'S NOT FOR YOU!"

The banging and clanging and chanting became almost deafening!

"Right, that's it, you've had your last chance!" bellowed The Grizzly Grumpot. He was shaking with rage as he yelled to Joscal and Tilano.

"Let's teach these stupid rebels a lesson!"

He pulled himself up to his very tallest height so that he was towering over the island folk and, with his sword waving dangerously, he bellowed, "Now you shall know the power of my anger! Don't say I didn't warn you!"

Then he faced the Grim-Groms and roared at them, "All of you, line up and get ready to charge!"

The Grim-Groms stood in a shoddy line and aimed their swords. The islanders braced themselves for the battle. The flimsy gardening tools they were holding were no match for the heavy swords glinting in the sunlight. A horrible clash of heavy metal against splitting wood was about to happen.

In the meantime, Reema continued to hide up in the tree nearby, shivering with fear as this shocking scene was unfolding. It's a complete mystery why, at that very moment, he looked towards poor Orion, but look at him he did. He thought the great bird must have a broken heart, stranded on top of The Clock Tower and unable to help in any way. Just as Reema was turning back to watch the battle commence, he thought he saw Orion move.

"Surely not!" he uttered in disbelief. He sat perfectly still and, with his big brown eyes, he studied the great bird carefully. Yes, he could see quite clearly now, Orion's wings *were* slowly unfolding.

"Sleeping salamanders and whizzing wombats! Why oh why didn't you wake up sooner?" He was so shocked, and then he thought, "What can I do now? I must try to save the day!"

With no time to lose, Reema bolted down from the tree like lightening and headed towards the crowded scene below. On one side of the village green stood the good people of Blue Sky Island. They were holding their simple wooden tools in defiance. On the other side were the threatening Grim-Groms with pointed swords in hand, ready for the battle. Their menacing master was still yelling at the top of his voice. Reema scampered onto the village green as fast as his furry little legs could carry him.

Tilano spotted him immediately and barked, "Hey look! There's that pesky squirrel! After him somebody! Catch him quick!"

Reema took no notice and squealed in his loudest voice, "Up! Up! Up! Everyone, you must look up. Up!!"

He continued to scamper along the middle pathway between the rumbling forces facing each other.

"Look up to The Clock Tower, look up! Come on everyone, look up, look up!!" He just kept on repeating the same thing.

Everybody turned their gaze to the Many-a-Moon Clock Tower, as Reema bolted back into the tree for safety.

The Grizzly Grumpot wasn't having any of it, thinking it was just another stupid diversion. He roared at the Grim-Groms to charge forward. To his dismay, not a single one of them moved. They were all transfixed to the spot, craning their short, stumpy necks up towards The Clock Tower with their mouths gaping open.

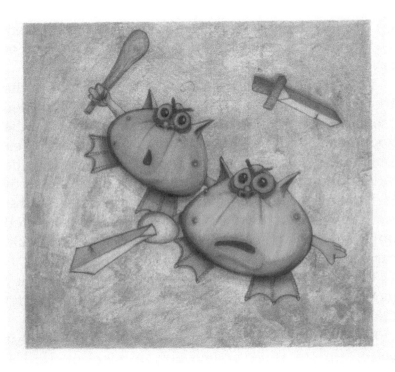

Alex and Ordompom were still chained together but Alex rattled his handcuffs and gasped out loud, "Oh look Ordompom! Look at what is happening!"

The Wizard peered over the top of his half glasses and his jaw dropped open. Orion was slowly but surely spreading his magnificent wings for all to see.

"The bird. He has awakened!" wailed Joscal to his master.

"This is *not* possible!" roared The Grizzly Grumpot, in a fit of fury.

"Orion, Orion, the magic is working after all," whispered Alex under his breath.

"This is meowvellous!" said Pusspom from inside the rusty cage.

As for Ordompom, he was too stunned to say anything at all and watched Orion gently stretching his wings in the sunlight.

"Look at Orion now. I think he's going to try and fly!" exclaimed Alex excitedly.

Sure enough, with a simple flap of his great wings, Orion took off from The Clock Tower that had been his home for so long. Into the air he soared and swooped and showed great pleasure in the joy of his newly found freedom. Then he glided over to the village green and circled above the amazed onlookers.

The Grizzly Grumpot watched this spectacle with a rage that was bubbling over like a witch's cauldron. The shocked islanders noticed steam coming out of his ears as he yelled at the Grim-Groms,

"You *will* attack these people at once, d'you hear me? We're goin' to show them WHO'S IN CHARGE!!"

The Grim-Groms just stood there quaking, as above them Orion circled with the Magic Orb wedged firmly in his talons. His piercing ruby red eyes stared at The Grizzly Grumpot and The Grizzly Grumpot glared right back at him.

A complete hush fell over the village green as this confrontation was taking place. Once again it became so quiet that you could almost hear a pin drop.

But then something extraordinary happened, which no one could quite believe. Even Alex, who was used to all the magical surprises on Blue Sky Island, was astounded. For at that moment, The Grizzly Grumpot who only a second ago had been fuming with rage, suddenly found he couldn't be angry anymore and started to smile from ear to ear. He exposed all of his dingy yellow teeth and let out a loud shriek of laughter with his stale and stinky breath.

"What ON EARTH is goin' on?" he exclaimed with a mystified chuckle.

Well he soon found out, for a merriment spell had been cast over him by Orion. The Golden Eagle still held on to the ancient power of the Magic Orb that Ord the Great had bestowed so many moons ago, and this was strong enough to make the spell work. Indeed, the spell was starting to work so well that The Grizzly Grumpot could not wipe the broad grin from his face, try as he may. He scratched his head in bewilderment and said with glee, "I don't want to be happy! I am *never* jolly or cheerful! I want to be bad, mad, horrid and sad!!"

And then he began to laugh out loud, "Ha-ha-ha! Oh Ha-ha-ha! Oh! Oh! Somebody help me!!"

The Grim-Groms were aghast at this dreadful spectacle as they watched their master howling with laughter. The Grizzly Grumpot hollered,

"This has got to stop at once! D'you hear me Orion! Oh Ha-ha-ha-ha-ha! Oh, oh my sides are splittin'!!" Orion ignored his plea and then, with his great wings spread, he hovered over the Grim-Groms.

"I wonder what he will do now?" whispered Ordompom in Alex's ear and before his very eyes he found out. As the Grim-Groms were looking up at Orion, slowly but surely the tips of their heavy pointed swords began to curl over. These dangerous weapons were slowly turning into bendy rubber and were now as useless as a piece of over-cooked spaghetti! When these pesky, mean and green creatures found they had nothing left to fight with, they flung down their rubbery swords and rolled about, chuckling and chortling because they were even more miserable than usual. When they'd exhausted themselves, they too scratched their heads because they didn't know what to do next.

Ordompom, Alex and the crowd of islanders stood and watched these goings-on in complete disbelief. Still clasping their gardening tools and ready for the fight, they were now faced with this bizarre scene instead.

Meanwhile Orion flew over to where Ordompom and Alex stood manacled together. The Magic Orb shimmered over them like fairy dust and, in a flash, their chains were gone! As for Pusspom sitting patiently in the rusty old cage, Orion flew past her and the cage disappeared in a puff of smoke! Pusspom calmly sat there licking her paw as though nothing had happened.

Ordompom stepped forward and spoke sternly to The Grizzly Grumpot. "Since you invaded our beautiful island, you have brought with you nothing but disaster and calamity. Our peaceful way of life and the happiness we enjoy has been gravely disrupted. Our crops are all but ruined and our animals have been harassed. You set up camp in amongst the ancient and protected trees of the Yellowood Woods and made a terrible mess. Your evil ways have not won you the right to stay here."

Ordompom picked up his large gardening fork and used it to point towards the coast.

"Now pack up your belongings and leave. Don't ever come back otherwise you shall have the wrath of Orion upon you once again."

"Ha-Ha-Ha, yes I will leave, yes I will, Ha-Ha-Ha! But for heaven's sake get that 'orrible bird to take this wretched spell orf me otherwise I will die laughin'! Ha-Ha-Ha!" shrieked The Grizzly Grumpot. And, with that, he fell flat on his back in a mass of blubbering guffaws, as the tears rolled down his face.

Dismayed, Joscal and Tilano went over to help get their master back on his feet. It was impossible as The Grizzly Grumpot was so exhausted from all that laughing, he just couldn't move. He was surrounded by the rest of the Grim-Groms, who came waddling up to help carry him away. Tilano shouted out a command, "Right then, let's do this. One, two, three and UP!" They had great difficulty in shifting The Grizzly Grumpot, for indeed he was very, very heavy!

The Grizzly Grumpot was still shrieking, "I will take my revenge on you someday, you'll see! Oh-Oh, Ha-Ha-Ha! You haven't seen the last of me!!"

Moving at a snail's pace the Grim-Groms staggered off under the weight of their half-crazy master and, eventually, this astonishing sight and the sound of the Grizzly Grumpot's mad laughter faded into the distance. The villagers stood there watching for a long time, until the invaders had well and truly gone. Ordompom clambered back onto the bench and held up his hand for quiet so that everyone could listen to what he had to say.

"We must give thanks to Orion for saving the day and ridding us of that loathsome villain. How glad we are to see the back of him! But now duty calls and Orion has to continue his journey to the Elder Wizard's Rest Home in the Sky. The protective powers of the Magic Orb must be renewed without fail. The delay has been far too great and he should leave immediately." Ordompom said that with great urgency in his voice.

The villagers nodded in agreement. Orion soared above them, high in the sky. He swooped down once more and looked at them all with his glittering ruby eyes. He still had the Magic Orb wedged firmly between his talons and every single person on the village green waved to him. Orion turned on the breeze and flew majestically away. Soon he was but a small speck on the horizon.

"Dear friend, do take care," sighed Ordompom. He and the others continued to wave goodbye until Orion had completely disappeared from view.

The islanders hugged each other and, one by one, they dropped their tools into the wheelbarrows, which were wheeled back to the gardening shed under the old oak tree. Drifting away from the village green and still talking about the battle that never happened, they all breathed a big sigh of relief. Orion had saved the day and now it was time to go home.

Chapter 16.

A Special Gift

Walking up the garden path and in through the front door, Ordompom couldn't wait to get out of his soggy clothes. Soon he emerged clean and dry in a blue checked shirt, green trousers and his favourite red star-spangled braces – the ones he'd been wearing when he first met Alex at Country Cottage.

"I'm feeling much better now," he said cheerfully.

He beckoned to Alex, Pusspom and Reema, "This is a most excellent and happy day after all that has happened. We should celebrate by having a picnic on the front lawn."

The others nodded in agreement and they got busy in the kitchen preparing tasty food – eggy sandwiches and cream cheese pinwheels, crunchy carrot and cucumber sticks and piccolo tomatoes. With a bowl of fresh strawberries and blueberries and some cherry-ade to drink, it was perfect ... and not forgetting some mashed sardines for Pusspom and a handful of cobnuts for Reema.

Everyone trooped into the garden. Alex carefully spread the red and white gingham tablecloth on the grass and they laid out all the goodies.

As Ordompom sat down he beamed at Alex and said, "For afters, you can have those delicious berries and

some butterscotch ice cream sprinkled with chocolate drops if you like. You jolly well deserve it!"

And that was exactly how Alex came to have his last meal on Blue Sky Island. On a perfect summer's day and spent with his new-found friends, together they chatted and laughed in the warm sunshine. Alex was happy to know there was nothing to worry about anymore.

At the very same time over on the north side of the island, a fleet of poddy paddle boats were hastily being filled with the shabby belongings of the Grim-Groms. The Grizzly Grumpot was busy loading up his mouldy old stuff too. He had finally stopped laughing and was stomping around as he cleared out his dingy hut. He grabbed the sack full of sparrow feathers, hedgehog quills and hay that had been his makeshift bed. He shook it hard and emptied it all over the floor.

"Let them clean up my mess, I'm out of here," he sneered.

Then he wandered down to the golden sandy beach where the boats were waiting and took a long last look at Blue Sky Island. With the sea so beautifully clear, even the colourful fish swimming in the bay darted away when they saw The Grizzly Grumpot coming. He was feeling bitter with regret and watched as the Grim-Groms threw their final junk into the heavily laden boats. With difficulty he clambered into the biggest boat of all. He shouted at them to cast off and the Grim-Groms struggled to push his hefty boat into the sparkling blue waters. The other boats followed behind him and they sailed away to who knows where, hopefully never to be seen again...

As the afternoon wore on, Alex knew his adventure was almost at an end. Ordompom spoke to him kindly,

"I really don't know what we would have done without you Alex. But the time has come for you to go home. I have used my Midi-Magic to call for Orion's Messenger and, with a bit of luck, he will be arriving here very soon."

He paused for a moment and looked at Alex with a twinkle in his eye.

"There is one more thing I have left to do."

With that, he reached into the front pocket of his shirt and took out a small item. Alex couldn't see what it was, because Ordompom's hand was tightly closed around it.

"I managed to 'magic up' something rather special just for you," said Ordompom with pride. He uncurled his fingers and there, nestling in the palm of his hand, sat a tiny ball that glittered brightly in the sunlight.

"This is a little 'thank you' for all your help. As you can see, it is a Mini Magic Orb and it will protect you and bring you good luck," smiled Ordompom.

Alex looked closely at the dazzling ball of light. It was no bigger than a marble and it sparkled just like the real thing. Ordompom handed the Mini Magic Orb to Alex.

"Take good care of it," he urged.

"Wow, this is the coolest present I have *ever* had!" said Alex with delight.

"It will remind you of a fantastical moment in time we shared together," said Ordompom, looking over the top of his half glasses.

Then he shook Alex's hand to say goodbye. As he was doing so, a gentle fluttering sound could be heard in the air and Alex turned round to find the giant falcon landing on the lawn. Orion's Messenger had come to take him home.

"Have a safe journey back to your kingdom," said Ordompom solemnly.

"Goodbye, we will miss you," purred Pusspom.

"You were great, you were just great!" piped Reema, twitching his bushy tail.

Alex walked across the grass and climbed onto the back of the great bird. He snuggled into the endless soft brown feathers for the return journey. Orion's Messenger spread out his wings and, in a few seconds, they were airborne once more. Alex looked down at the enchanted island and the quaint little cottage where his friends were waving goodbye. Soon they were but tiny dots in the distance and Alex settled down for the long journey ahead.

Chapter 17.

A New Day Dawns

"Alex, Alex, it's time to wake up," said his mother, shaking him gently.

"Please go away," he mumbled sleepily.

"It's the first day of term, don't you remember?"

"Oh no, it's far too early," Alex groaned and promptly fell sleep again. His mother stood in the doorway, surprised at how quickly he had dropped off. She spoke to him in a louder voice.

"Alex, Alex you must wake up. Come on now, it really is time to get washed and dressed." She pulled at his duvet, this time with more insistence.

"Oh, okay, I'll be out of bed in a minute or two," he mumbled from under his pillow.

"Don't be long then," she urged, and left the bedroom.

Alex lay there listening to his bedside clock which was ticking far too loudly. Then he yawned and slowly, but surely, he sat up and stretched. Something wasn't quite right as he looked around him with his eyes half closed. He tried to work out what was puzzling him, but he was so tired he couldn't think straight. He rolled out of bed and stumbled into the bathroom to splash his face with some cold water.

"That's a bit better," he said, looking at his weary reflection in the mirror.

He started to get dressed and it suddenly dawned on him why he was so tired. He'd had the best dream ever, which seemed never ending. Yes, it was all coming back to him now. The flight on the back of the splendid falcon to a magical island in the sun. Talking cats and fluffy squirrels, and a kindly old wizard, who wasn't very good at casting spells. Oh, so much to remember. There was a busy marketplace and some friendly islanders and then he recalled the old wizard as he went flying through the air to the top of the tallest clock tower ever! And as for that nasty, grizzly, bad-tempered beast who was being followed around by some strange green creatures with flaming orange eyes, oh my goodness me! Alex then frowned as he thought about the battle that never was. He didn't like that bit of his dream, but then he smiled to himself at the wilting rubbery swords and that ghastly laughing beast being carried off into the distance. The very best part of his dream though, featured the magnificent Golden Eagle who held a dazzling ball of light in his talons. What an amazing night of adventure it had been.

"I can't wait to get to school and tell Reuben and Manny all the things I dreamt about last night. It seemed so real, but then I woke up..."

He paused and had a wishful thought, "It was such a magical world, I wonder if I will ever dream about it again."

His thoughts were interrupted when his mother called up from the kitchen, "Breakfast is on the table."

"I'm nearly ready," he yelled back.

He put on his shirt and trousers, fastened his shoes and straightened his school tie. Finally, he went over to the large chest of drawers standing in the corner of his bedroom. Sitting on top of the chest he found a new bus pass, which his mother had left out for him. He put it into his trouser pocket and, as he did so, Alex was aware of something in there already.

"That's strange," he thought, "There shouldn't be anything in these trousers, they're brand new."

Wrapping his hand around the small item in his pocket, he carefully took it out and gave a loud gasp. He couldn't believe what he was looking at. Right there, in his hand, sat something small and sparkling. Something that looked remarkably like ... the Mini Magic Orb.

Lightning Source UK Ltd.
Milton Keynes UK
UKHW021033100321
380089UK00007B/269